Molly's New Song

BRIDES OF
PELICAN RAPIDS

Elaine Manders

Scripture references are taken from the King James Version (KJV) of the Bible.

Cover Design: Evelyn Labelle, Carpe Librum Book Design

Also special thanks to my fellow authors in the Brides of Pelican Rapids Series for their encouragement and contribution to this series.

May every reader be blessed and the Lord be magnified.

Message to Readers

Dear Reader

Thank you for buying my books, reading them, and supporting Christian fiction—even if you just like a clean romance. Your cards, letters, emails, and reviews lift my spirit and motivate me to write the next book.

If you would like to join the team to support this series, here is the link.

https://www.facebook.com/groups/877959952547231/

To get first-hand information about upcoming releases, have input to new books, join our parties for prizes and fun, and meet the authors. Subscribe to my newsletter at https://dl.bookfunnel.com/or10xrsvje, and receive a free novella.

It's better to light one small candle than to curse the darkness. I believe the Lord will bless our efforts to improve the culture through literature, even in this small way.

Be sure to check out all of my books.

https://www.amazon.com/Elaine-Manders/e/B0116MKKJG/ref=sr_tc_2_0?qid=1524173840&sr=1-2-ent

Oh, sing to the Lord a new song. Sing to the Lord, all the earth. Sing to the Lord, bless His name. Proclaim the good news of His salvation from day to day. Declare His glory among the nations. His wonders among all peoples.

-Psalm 96: 1-3

Chapter 1

Honor your father and your mother, as the Lord your God has commanded you, that it may be well with you in the land which the Lord your God is giving you. Deuteronomy 5:16

Molly Stewart peered from her bedroom window. Yes, that was Daddy who'd slammed the broken gate. Which meant he was already in a foul mood. She sighed and dropped the blue percale curtains, threadbare from many washings, doing nothing to keep out the oppressive Georgia sun.

He had a good reason to be despondent. Before the War Between the States he'd been one of the most successful planters in the State. But he, like all the other landowners, had lost everything in Sherman's horrific march to the sea.

Now, eight years later, most of their neighbors had been able to pick up the pieces and fashion a new life out of the fragments left them. But not Daddy. He'd jumped from one scheme to another, believing the cruel scoundrels who promised riches. The Carpetbaggers, those who came from the North to pick over the remains of the ravaged towns and the Scallywags, Southerners who teamed up with them. The riches fell to them, not those they deceived.

She hated to admit Daddy was gullible, but he'd finally hit the bottom, having lost the overseer's cottage, their home after the plantation house burned, along with the rest of the land.

Oh, how she hated to think of the beautiful place this had once been. Or that Stephen, her older brother, had been killed in his first battle. Or that Mama had died—the greatest loss of all.

The front door closed, not a slam, but a little harder than necessary.

Poor Daddy. Now she had to give him more bad news. She snatched the letter from her bedside table and, hiking her skirts, bounded down the stairs.

Daddy sent no glance her way as she hit the last step. Instead he turned in a wide circle, studying the parlor. "Something is different in here." He glared at her. "Something is missing."

"Hello to you, too, Daddy. You're back from the bank earlier than I'd expected, or I would have gotten supper started." She just now realized the time. He wasn't all that early. Thankfully. She strode towards the kitchen. Maybe her news would set better on a full stomach.

"The piano," he bellowed. The words stopped her. So much for supper. "Your piano is missing."

She retraced her steps. "Yes, I know."

"You sold it? I told you we'd take it with us to Sadie's. She'd pitch a fit. Never liked music, but I gained that one concession when I told her it was your mother's piano—the only thing of value left from the fire." He moved in wide strides, closing the distance between them. "And now you've sold it?"

"No, Daddy. I didn't sell it. I could never do that."

"Then where is it?"

She laid a hand on his arm. "We need to talk." She ambled to the sofa and waited for him to follow.

This was like she was twelve years old again, and Mama caught her reading a dime novel. Being called on the carpet to be upbraided to confess her sins.

Except Mama wasn't here now and she was a grown woman, intending to stand up for her decision. "The day after my twenty-fourth birthday, I was sitting in here, playing the piano when I felt the Lord speaking to me. Seemed to me He was telling me I wasn't given the gift of music to entertain myself. In fact, I wasn't created to serve one cantankerous old woman. I wasn't meant to go through life alone."

"What are you saying?"

"Daddy, I can't go to Aunt Sadie's. It isn't that she's...difficult. She lives way out in the sticks, and she'll expect me to be her servant while begrudging you and me every bite we eat. If I go, I'll be waiting on her until the day she dies—or I do from boredom." Surely Daddy could understand her reasoning. Aunt Sadie might make allowances for him to indulge in his passion for fishing and hunting. What else did the countryside offer in those isolated woods of south Alabama?

"I may be an old maid, but I want to think I have some future. Something to live for."

"Old maid?" Daddy laughed. "You're not an old maid."

"In four months I'll be twenty-five years old.

That's an old maid by anyone's standards. Besides, I have no skills except playing the piano. Who around here can afford to hire me to teach their children to play?"

"Of course not. Hiring yourself out for anything is beneath you."

But it wasn't beneath her to eat. To wish for a home of her own. A husband. Children.

Despite selling out and agreeing to move in with Aunt Sadie, Daddy hadn't accepted their reduced circumstances.

"If you didn't sell the piano, where is it?"

"It's on its way to Minnesota."

Daddy's eyes threatened to pop out of their sockets. "You sold it to Yankees?"

"I didn't *sell* it. I'm going to Minnesota myself. See—"

Daddy got choked. She pounded him on the back and went on before he got his voice back. "I applied to Mrs. Milton's agency to become a mail-order bride, and she matched me with a wonderful young farmer. His name is Luke Ferrell, and he's a—"

He snatched the paper out of her hand. "You what? You signed a contract to marry a Yankee?"

"Mrs. Milton is a wonderful woman and takes great care to find her brides suitable Christian mates. See—she has all these recommendations." She pointed to the glowing reports of Mrs. Milton's happy brides who'd found the love of their lives.

"I won't allow it." Daddy boomed. "I've told you I'll find you a husband. It's just more difficult since so many young men of suitable age and standing were killed in that cursed war. You just have to be patient."

"Where will you find a suitable mate for me in the boondocks of southern Alabama?"

"I'm sure Sadie knows someone."

"Aunt Sadie doesn't know anyone under the age of sixty, and she wants me to be her maid since she's run off the last three."

"We still have a week here. I'll find someone much more suitable than a Yankee. After all, a Georgia dirt farmer is better than a Yankee dirt farmer. I can't believe you'd do this after refusing Harlan Hightower."

"Harlan Hightower is almost as old as you, Daddy."

"Well, it won't be hard to find someone else. You're a beautiful young woman."

"Daddy, you're prejudiced and believe me, there's no one available. I've looked. And I've corresponded with Mr. Ferrell. He's a fine Christian man. Would you like to see his picture?"

He held out a hand to block her before she'd even managed to retrieve the picture. "No—and I want you to write this man and tell him you'll not be coming. That your father needs you. And I do."

Here it came. The piling on of guilt where he reminded her—

"You're all I have left, Molly. I lost my son. My Agnes. How can I possibly stand Sadie without you? Haven't I lost enough? The good Lord wouldn't let me lose you. And to a Yankee? Have you forgotten how much we lost to them?"

"Daddy, the good Lord would want us to forgive."

He gave no sign of having heard her.

Chapter 2

He who finds a wife finds a good thing. And obtains favor from the Lord. Proverbs 18:22.

Pelican Rapids was bustling when Luke Farrell drove his buckboard on Main Street. He hadn't been to town in over a month. Not after he'd received Molly Stewart's answer to his proposal, and the smile hadn't left his face since.

He'd check at the post office to make sure Molly had received the tickets and, since he was running low on supplies, he'd have to stop by the mercantile too. For once he wouldn't have to worry about Mrs. Carter pushing off one of her daughters on him.

Luke found the postmaster, Gus, with his back to the door, sorting mail. Gus lifted a hand asking for silence until he'd finished whatever task he was at. Luke waited patiently, and after a couple of minutes, Gus glanced over his shoulder.

Without even asking, he reached into a box and pulled out an envelope. "This what you looking for?" He peered at Luke from under bushy brows and a grin twitched his equally bushy moustache. Gus rarely ever smiled so it must be from Molly. The postmaster, like everyone in Pelican Rapids, knew Luke was planning to marry a mail-order bride from Georgia.

Luke grabbed the envelope, the rose scent telling him without even looking at the address this came from Molly. His heart raced as he tore it open. There was always the possibility she'd changed her mind. Finding no tickets inside, he released a sigh. Since she hadn't returned the tickets, she had to be on her way.

Her lovely, feminine handwriting, so familiar to him, swam before his eyes. He forced himself to focus on the short missive. The words seemed rushed, unlike her previous letters, but they conveyed what he wanted to know. She'd be arriving next week.

His pulse kicked up another notch.

She'd added a post script. *You wrote in your first letter that you were getting ready to paint your house and asked my opinion. It occurs to me I forgot to answer. I simply love yellow houses with green shutters and trim.*

Yellow? Green? Shutters?

"Guess it's all settled?" Gus broke into his thoughts.

"I haven't finished the house. She wants it painted."

"Painted? Most folks just let the house weather. You got all the repairs done?"

"I finished all except for a few repairs." Not to mention making shutters.

He'd spent the better part of the spring planting season working on the house, barn, and corral. Replacing rotted boards, cleaning out old hay, scrubbing walls and floors.

Molly was raised a well-to-do lady, and though she'd related how hard it was to make do with what little was left of her father's once great plantation, she'd probably be expecting a lot more than his little place.

Luke had only one regret about his bride-to-be.

He didn't mind she was a Southerner. Several Southern ladies had come as brides to his neighbors. They were all lovely women who'd settled in well with the local population.

He just wished Molly came from any other State than Georgia.

Luke had served in the army, fought against the Confederacy. He'd always thought the cause was noble. Still did. Nothing about war left pleasant memories, but when you faced an enemy, you had to fight.

The regiment he'd served in Georgia was different. Maybe they were war weary, but seemed to him the leaders went crazy. Looting and burning in a way that sickened Luke and left him praying to be reassigned, and he'd finally succeeded. But he didn't want to think about that.

His orders to leave the army came a few months before the end of the war, and he'd been able to put those memories far behind him. Would Molly be a constant reminder?

Guilt gnawed at him because he'd lied to Molly. He'd written that he'd never been in Georgia.

But he didn't want to dreg up that dark past, and he'd done his best to forget about the war and only look to the future. And where his wife was born had no bearing on how they'd live, the future they'd forge here in this quiet, peaceful country. The family they'd raise would know nothing of war.

Just the thought of future children brought the blood rushing to his face. Unless Molly took one look at his poor little farm and high-tailed it back south. No, she wouldn't do that, although he wished he'd explained his circumstances better to her.

"You all right, Luke?" Gus asked, looking concerned. "A man getting married shouldn't look that flushed."

"You better believe I'm all right. Nothing but good news." He waved the letter. "She'll be arriving next Saturday."

Gus came from behind the counter, all smiles, and stretched out a hand. "Congratulations. I'm happy for you and her. She's getting a good man."

Luke laughed to release some of the joy. He must be acting like a yokel. Well, he was a yokel, but Molly was a lady, and he'd work his fingers to the bone to deserve her. "I don't know about that, but she's getting a happy man."

He didn't even feel the boardwalk under his boots as he strode to the mercantile. He wanted to holler out at everyone on this side of the street and the other that he was getting married.

Finally, they'd probably think. They all knew how unlucky he'd been in love.

When he'd returned to his parents' home in Illinois, after the war, the sweetheart who'd been waiting for him—sweet Daisy—was stricken with consumption. She'd refused to marry him, knowing she didn't have long to live. She'd died before the first frost of sixty-six. Then Barbara had come along and left him for another man. But that was something he couldn't tell Molly until they were married and had grandchildren. Maybe not then.

He'd worked on his parents' farm until Grandpa died, leaving him his spread outside Pelican Rapids. That was two years ago. He'd found the place in poor condition. After Grandma had passed away, Grandpa had lost all interest in keeping the farm up and eked out only enough to support himself and his few livestock.

The familiar smell of kerosene, leather, tobacco, and fresh bolts of fabric hit him as he entered the empty mercantile. He waited just inside the door to give his eyes a chance to adjust from the bright sunlight to the store's dim interior. Couldn't the Carters afford better lighting?

He fished inside his pocket for his list and approached the vacant counter. A slap of the bell brought Mrs. Carter at a trot. "Luke Ferrell. I have wonderful news about Mandy, and I was hoping you'd come in today. Now you don't go nowhere. I'll give this list to the mister to fill." She glanced at the roll of rope on the wall like she wanted to hog tie him to the counter.

Now why would he leave? He already knew the wonderful news about Mandy.

Luke considered Mandy Carter a good friend, and she felt the same way as far as he knew. She'd credited him with giving her the courage to escape her domineering parents by going on an extended visit to her grandparents in New York. Mandy had written him last month to announce that she was getting married to the dentist who'd fixed her teeth. He'd been meaning to write Mandy about his Molly.

Mrs. Carter returned, a big smile on her round face. "Mandy's coming home next week."

"That's nice. It'll be good to see her again." He reached into the candy jar on the counter and popped a licorice stick in his mouth.

"I knew you'd feel that way. We mean to have a dinner to welcome her back, and of course, you must come. I feel like Mandy's ready to settle down now. Mr. Carter and I want you to know you have our blessings to start courting right away."

He almost choked on the licorice. When he got his breath back, he said, "I thought she was getting married to her dentist in New York."

Mrs. Carter laughed and slapped him on the chest. "Oh, that. It was all a big mistake. Why, Mr. Carter and I couldn't let her marry somebody so far from home. We might never see her again."

Luke dropped the licorice stick in the waste basket. Somehow, he didn't think it was the right time to tell Mrs. Carter his mail-order bride was coming in next week, and he wouldn't be available to court Mandy. Especially since he needed her help.

"It'll be nice to see her again. Do you have any yellow or green paint?"

Mrs. Carter drew back like he might be dangerous. "We have some yellow and red...and white, of course. No green. Why in the world would you need yellow and green paint?"

"You know I built a wood clapboard house beside my grandparents' soddy? I decided to paint it." He chuckled. "The house, not the soddy."

She nodded, knowingly. "Mandy told me about that. She didn't have to tell me why. I don't remember her favoring either yellow or green, though."

"I'd like to try it. I suppose the yellow costs more than whitewash."

"Quite a bit, I'm afraid."

"I'll take a gallon and mix it with the whitewash I have left. That should be enough."

Mrs. Carter wrinkled her nose like she'd gotten a whiff of horse manure. "You really need a larger house when you get married, Luke. It's hardly big enough to cuss a cat. I don't know how Mandy can manage in that tiny place."

He'd have loved to build a bigger house, but money was tight. He turned around to inspect the garden tools hanging on the wall, not because he needed any new implements, but he needed some time to think of a way to straighten out Mrs. Carter's misunderstanding without her having a fit. He glanced over his shoulder. "I intend to build on after harvest."

Mrs. Carter's brows arched with unconcealed annoyance. "I doubt Mandy would want to wait that long." She huffed. "But I have a chart about mixing dyes. It says you can get green by mixing yellow and blue."

He whirled around. "Really? That might work."

"I don't have any blue paint, but we do carry blue fabric dye. Don't know why you couldn't use that. Color is color."

He laughed. "That's right. Glad you mentioned it. I wouldn't have thought of that. Add two gallons of yellow paint and a package of blue dye to my supply list. I'll be back to pick everything up in a little while."

He got out of there before she could mention any more about Mandy, though he was curious why Mandy had called off her marriage.

A ruckus down at the depot drew his attention. A crowd had gathered. Must be about half of

Pelican Rapids standing around the street, making him wonder if there was a visiting dignitary like when President Grant came through. He had the time. Might as well see what was going on.

Talking and laughter grew louder as he approached. Ben Johnson, standing on the depot platform, caught his eye. "Hey, Luke," he yelled above the noise, "better get over here and see this."

The crowd parted like the Red Sea, revealing a—

Piano?

The biggest piano Luke had ever seen. Shaped funny too. But it had to be a piano. Luke had seen one in the saloon. Not that he visited the saloon too often, but he'd had to go in one day to drag Link Markham out for his wife. And he'd always heard the piano being played when he happened to pass that part of town at night. Playing tunes like *Camptown Ladies, Oh Susanna, Buffalo Gals*.

No sir, this piano put the saloon piano to shame. It was spread out with curving sides and made of gleaning Cherrywood. But it had piano keys across the front.

Mrs. Carter came hustling behind him, breathing heavy. She pushed her way through the crowd. "It's a piano." She looked at him like she was explaining to a three-year-old.

"I know it's a piano, but why was it delivered to me? I sure didn't order a—" He drew in a breath.

Molly.

Somewhere in one of her ten-page letters she'd mentioned something about wishing she could bring her piano. But he'd dismissed that as wishful musing. She'd also written it cost too much, and Mrs. Milton hadn't sent her enough money to freight a piano.

He scratched his head, still wondering how he could have misunderstood Molly's intentions. She'd also mentioned she wished she could bring the magnolia tree outside her bedroom window. He could've handled the magnolia tree. He had plenty of yard, though a magnolia tree would die during its first harsh Minnesota winter.

The porter brought him a fistful of papers. He laid them on the piano's glossy top. "Here you go, Mr. Ferrell. Sign here." He shoved a pencil in Luke's face and pointed to the top paper. "It came all the way from Georgia, and not a scratch on it."

"Yeah, it's from Molly, uh, that is, Miss Stewart." Luke took the pencil and signed the document.

"Who's Molly?" Mrs. Carter was at his elbow.

"So, what are you going to do with it, son?" Mr. Lemon asked.

Luke rubbed his neck. "If I can get a couple of you men to help me get it on my buckboard, I'll take it out to the farm."

"It'll take four men at least. That thing's got to

weigh a ton." Sheriff Alton Kouch slapped him on the back. "Guess I need to round up a piano posse." He tipped his Stetson back to peer at the sky. "Looks like it might rain."

"I'd appreciate that, Sheriff. Molly will be mighty upset if her piano gets wet."

Mrs. Carter got in his face. "Who is Molly?"

"She's my mail-order bride." He could have bit his tongue as soon as the words flew out, but now that they had, maybe he could slam a door on the quarrelsome woman's match-making plans. "Coming all the way from Georgia. You're invited to the wedding, Mrs. Carter." He swept a glance around the crowd. "Everyone is."

Mrs. Carter turned three shades of red. "What!" She held up a fist like she might throttle him. "What about your understanding with Mandy? How could you do this to her?" She shouted loud enough for everyone to hear.

He replied just as loud but had the sense to take a step back. "Mandy and I didn't have an understanding, Mrs. Carter. We were nothing more than friends. She said in her last letter she was getting married to that dentist back east."

"But I told you she's not." Mrs. Carter tried to block his way.

He stepped around her. "Excuse me. I have to pull my buckboard up here." Would there be room on the buckboard with all his supplies after they got the piano loaded?

Chapter 3

Thy God is with thee whitersoever thou goest.
Josiah 1:9

Molly couldn't believe she was doing this. Sneaking out in the middle of the night to run away. But what choice did she have? It was conceivable Daddy would attempt to physically stop her from leaving.

And leave she must. Tonight. She had to be on that train tomorrow morning. True, she should have confronted Daddy sooner, persuaded him this was best for her. Given time, Daddy would have come around. He loved her and wanted the best for her. Always had. Trouble was, he didn't think marrying a Yankee was best for her.

Her surreptitious leaving was causing all sorts of problems. She'd have to walk. Didn't dare take Sulkie, the sorrel mare she'd had since Sulkie was a filly and Molly just toddling. She'd actually wept when she'd taken the horse some sugar cubes a little while ago and said her good-byes. Sulkie seemed to understand what she meant to do because she'd tried to follow Molly.

It wasn't likely she'd even have a horse in Minnesota. Didn't farmers prefer mules? Certainly, they didn't keep horses for a lady to ride for pleasure. A farmer's wife didn't have time for such luxuries.

But she was used to hard work. She knew what she was getting into, the sacrifices she had to make. Even facing unknowns in an unknown land she knew God would go with her. The Spirit within her would guide the way.

The years of depravities had brought her closer to God. The years since they'd lost the plantation, and then the land, had forced her to do without luxuries. She'd learned to wash and sew her own clothes, clean her own house, cook for herself and Daddy. As money got scarcer, she'd taught the neighbor's children piano. There weren't many students to be had, but the few dollars she'd received from their better-off parents had stretched hers and Daddy's provisions through several winters.

She recalled her mammy, standing before her, hands on her ample hips, saying, "You got to do what you got to do, and iffn you don't do it, little missy, you'll do without."

Dear, wise Mammy. She'd left right after the war mercifully ended with the rest of them, though she'd written Molly several times since. Actually, one of her relatives had written for her because Mammy had never learned to read or write. She'd moved to Illinois. That wasn't so far from Minnesota. Maybe Molly could visit her.

She packed the two carpetbags she intended to take with as many clothes and personal items as she could stuff inside. She'd intended to take the big trunk, but there was no way she could lug that thing all the way to town.

Even the carpetbags, fitted with leather shoulder slings, would test her strength. She rolled up her wedding gown–Mama's gown. The lace had turned yellow, but it was still a beautiful dress. Tears had welled in her eyes when she'd tried it on, and she wanted to believe Mama would be looking down from heaven on her wedding day.

She stuffed one of her two good dresses, a buttercup yellow of fine linen that looked so well with her dark hair. She wore the other, a fashionable blue gown she'd sewn this year, made from the silk and trim of old dresses.

A glance at the clock told her she must hurry. She frantically piled in two old dresses that would be useful for house and yard work. Then emptied her dresser drawers of her underclothes and quickly stuffed them into the other carpetbag.

With hand to her forehead, she scanned the room. She just knew she'd forgotten something, but time was running short. Nothing remained in sight except her old kid gloves, but they wouldn't look right with her fancy blue dress.

She stretched out her hands before her. They were red and calloused from washing clothes and dishes, her nails filed short from breaking. But Luke knew she wasn't a lady of leisure. She'd been honest with him.

Her heart pounding like a hammer against her ribs, she ran to the mirror for a final check. Her face was a complete contrast to her hands. Complexion lightly tanned with not a hint of a freckle was her best feature. Her curly, mahogany hair, two or three shades lighter than black, enhanced her looks. She'd tried to put her hair up but didn't have enough pins, so had tied it back with a ribbon.

Gently lifting the hat Daddy had given her for her last birthday, Molly set it on her unruly hair and smiled at her reflection. She looked as well as she could. That was a relief. Maybe Luke wouldn't even notice her hands. She didn't want Luke to be ashamed of her for anything.

The tin-type she'd sent him was of a sixteen-year-old, carefree girl. She hoped he wouldn't be disappointed at the way eight years of hard living had changed her looks. Her face now revealed the planes and shadows of a mature woman, but the same spark shone in her eyes.

The photograph Luke had sent her had to be of his younger self since he'd been in Union uniform. Thank goodness she'd refrained from showing Daddy.

Molly had asked Luke in one of her letters where he'd served in the army, wondering if he'd ever been in Georgia. He'd replied that he never had, but was vague about where he did serve. It was just as well she supposed. While she'd run on and on in her letters, Luke was a man of few words.

But a husband and wife should complement each other, shouldn't they?

She turned from the mirror and hooked her reticule. It sagged heavily on her wrist, owing to the odds and ends she couldn't do without, including the derringer lying in the bottom. Daddy had given it to her a couple of years ago, but she'd never fired it. And she prayed she wouldn't have to.

Did she even dare pray for God's protection on her trek to town? She was surely breaking one of His commandments. *Honor thy father and mother.* But was it really dishonoring her father to go against his wishes? *A man shall leave his father and mother and cleave unto his wife.* The same must apply to a woman. She'd have to leave her parents to cleave to her husband. Of course, that presupposed she'd have her parents blessing.

As she passed Daddy's bedroom, his snores soothed her conscience. She pressed a hand over the closed door.

Good-bye, Daddy. Please understand.

She passed through the kitchen, and laid the three-page letter she'd written at Daddy's place at the table. With one final look, she slipped out the backdoor.

As she got underway along the well-worn path to town, the almost full moon lit the way, but clouds passed over from time to time, throwing her in total darkness. Even so, she didn't stop. She could walk this road blindfolded.

The carpetbag straps bored into her shoulders by the time she'd covered half the distance, forcing her to stop and adjust them. Normally, she would walk to town in little more than an hour, but with the heavy load she carried, almost two hours had passed before she saw the first lights of Juliette.

The roosters were crowing when she reached the outskirts of town, and unfortunately, she had to enter at the derelict side of town. A dog barked, but she and the dog had become acquainted and she ignored it.

The street itself looked sinister, though the first lavender threads of dawn lightened the sky. Sounds of the awakening town reached her ears before she saw anything. Distant shouts, animals snorting, doors slamming. Fog filtered the light coming from the nearby buildings, including the saloon.

She tapped down the fear rising in her throat. Troublemakers would be sleeping off their drink by this time of morning.

The clip-clop of horses' hooves coming from behind startled her, and she scurried to the edge of the road. The carriage stopped.

The sign painted on the carriage door proclaimed it to be a public conveyance. She didn't even know there were such things in Juliette. Pressing a hand to her heart, she drew in the first relieved breath she'd spared since leaving home.

"Need a lift, ma'am?"

It would cost some of her precious coins but well worth saving her from walking through the town to the depot. She'd stick out like a rose in a field of cotton, and all eyes would be on her. Indeed, she must look strange to this driver. Like someone running away—or worse. Like a lady of the evening. "I would, kind sir," she said, her face burning.

Bless the man, he wasn't one to dwell into the private affairs of his customers. He jumped from the driver's seat and held the carriage door open for her. "Where to, ma'am?"

"The train depot. I must catch the seven o'clock train." She could tell from his speech he was from the North, probably a carpetbagger, as some would call him. There were those who judged all Northerners harshly, and Molly knew why hate festered in the hearts of many Southerners. Hatred for Yankees and the freedmen and women. It was hard for her to forget all she'd lost, but she also knew hatred would eat away at the soul of the hater and harden the heart.

This man might be a carpetbagger, but he was a welcome sight to her.

He nodded, and sent an upward glance to the sky. "You'll have time for breakfast at the café next door to the depot, and I recommend it. You won't find good food on the trains."

"Thank you, I intend to do just that." After relinquishing the heavy bags to the driver, she entered the carriage's dark interior and stretched her aching muscles.

The conveyance lurched forward, and her

stomach rumbled as she contemplated the pancakes smothered in sorghum syrup with ham and eggs the café had on its breakfast menu. She gazed out the window at the still dusky sky. Daddy was likely still snoring. He stayed up late at night reading and brooding and slept late in the morning. He'd awake to an empty house, a cold kitchen. That would be his first clue she was missing. He wouldn't smell her coffee.

But she'd convinced herself this move was best for Daddy, too. Of course she loved Daddy to pieces, but he'd come to lean on her too much, like he'd always leaned on Mama. They'd both given him too much sympathy, accepted his weaknesses too readily, made excuses for him. One thing was for sure. He wouldn't get any sympathy from Aunt Sadie. Maybe Aunt Sadie was just what he needed to spur him to leave the past behind and build a future for himself.

He wasn't too old to get married again—and there was a plethora of widows in the South. With Molly out of the way, he might look for someone.

One of the things that attracted her to Luke Ferrell was his strength. In his short letters, she'd seen him as a man who'd always had to make his own way, and not only that, he was willing to lend a helping hand to those around him. Helping his father expand his business after the war, then building up the farm his grandparents had left him while helping his neighbors with one emergency or another. It wasn't what he'd said in so many words, but she'd read between the lines.

The carriage halted at the depot. The nice driver carried her bags to the luggage area. Thanking him, she handed him the fare plus what she hoped was a decent tip. She had precious little money left after paying the freight on her piano, but it was unthinkable that she could leave it.

That piano was her heart, and when she played the old hymns her mother had taught her, she could feel Mama's sweet presence. Only then was that empty spot in her soul filled.

The train was already waiting, though it would be another hour before it left the station. The train that would take her to Luke.

Chapter 4

Now to Him who is able to do exceedingly abundantly above all that we ask or think, according to the power that works in us. To Him be glory in the church by Christ Jesus to all generations, forever and ever. Ephesians 3:20-21

Luke scrubbed a thick cotton handkerchief across his brow. Sure was hot today, even with the sun getting ready to dip under the tree line.

He washed up at the pump and entered the house through the back. The kitchen's familiar smell set his stomach rumbling. He'd brought a couple of ham sandwiches from town. Coffee would taste good, but no need to heat up the kitchen just for that.

What would it be like to have a wife to greet him at the end of the day? Dinner already waiting, and better than that, a smile and conversation to share the events of the day. He'd do his best to show an interest in her activities. Sewing, visiting neighbors. And after dinner, she'd play the piano.

If she could get in there.

He rounded the dining table and stopped in the entry to the parlor. Thankfully, he didn't have much furniture to begin with. A sofa, a matching wingchair, a side table. But as little as he had, it was now all bunched up along one wall. The piano was placed right between the fireplace and the front window—shoved up against it so close, it would've caught fire, if there was a fire.

He walked through the narrow space between sofa and piano and hit his knee against the piano bench.

Clearly, the piano would have to be moved before fall brought a chill to the air. He'd have to move the dining table, which he'd made himself from nearby oaks, to the old sod house, and put the piano in the dining room. He and Molly would have to dine at the small kitchen table.

Obviously, Molly had the impression his house was larger than it was. Had he misled her? He had bragged about building a new house to replace his grandparents soddy, but it never occurred to him she'd think it big enough for a piano. Hadn't she explained she'd become acclimated to living in the small overseer's cottage? And since the servants had all left, it was a good thing since the cottage was small enough for her to manage by herself. Still, the cottage was large enough for her piano.

And his farmhouse wasn't. No two ways about it.

He rubbed his neck and huffed a sigh. It would be easy enough to extend the house out ten or twelve feet—all the way across. Wouldn't even have to change the pitch of the roof. He glanced to the west wall. He could build it within a couple of months if the wedding was delayed that long. Mrs. Milton always expected her brides to stay with her for a while to get better acquainted with the groom.

But where would the money come from? He'd already used his meager savings in building the house. The size dictated by the amount he had to spend. He'd vowed not to go into debt. Taking out a mortgage before the farm was producing an excess seemed irresponsible. A trait he'd learned from his father who had never gone into debt in his life and had managed to make a comfortable living for his family.

Here in Minnesota, Luke's cultivated acreage of alfalfa and wheat was barely enough to see him through the winter. Now he'd have a wife to support. Possibly children. Yes, Molly had mentioned several times she wanted children and as soon as possible.

Truth was, he did too.

Maneuvering to the window, he hit his shin on the side table. Pain shot up his leg, but he ignored it and raised the window. He stuck his head out to get a view of the full length of the house. If it were extended all the way, there would be room for another bedroom. Right beside his and Molly's. The perfect place for a nursery.

His stomach growled, reminding him his ham sandwiches waited.

After eating, he sat at his little desk and drew up plans for the extension. Then he examined his bank book. Yep, it would take a mortgage which, for a farmer, was so risky. He'd pray about it and sleep on it. A decision would have to be made by tomorrow.

He'd stepped out on faith when he asked Mrs. Milton to find him a wife. If the Lord could do that, surely He would provide a way to build a bigger house.

One thing was for sure, he'd have to make room

for that piano.

Chapter 5

Bear ye one another's burdens. Galatians 6-2

The Chicago depot was a nightmare of confusion. And loud. Trains belching, hawkers yelling, whistles blowing. Molly stood stunned, looking in one direction and the other, trying to get the attention of someone. But people rushing in all directions ignored her.

Which gate to take? Her ticket didn't say. She assumed her luggage was going on the right train. Too bad no one had tagged her.

She noticed a young woman standing in front of the schedules and threaded her way in that direction. The lady looked to be about the same age as Molly and alone. "Excuse me, can you tell where I might go to get the connection going to Pelican Rapids, Minnesota?"

The woman jumped, shooting an eye-popping stare at Molly. Her mouth hung open like Molly had asked her directions to the moon. "You're going to Pelican Rapids?"

"Y...yes. Is there something wrong about that?"

The woman shook her head. "No, I'm going to Pelican Rapids myself. It's just that's such a small town, it's unusual to find a fellow passenger with the same destination." She reached out a hand. "I'm Mandy Carter. Pleased to meet you."

Molly smiled. "Molly Stewart. You're an answer to my prayers, Mandy. I was just asking God to send someone to help me through this labyrinth." She gripped Mandy's hand.

"Our train doesn't leave for almost an hour. That's just enough time to get a cold lemonade, and I know there's a stand just around the corner." Mandy flashed a smile that revealed a gold tooth in the corner of her mouth, right before the molars began. "Mandy and Molly—we're going to be great friends." She hooked Molly by the arm and swept her along the crowded corridor. What a lovely, friendly person Mandy was.

There was nowhere to sit to enjoy their lemonade, so they hugged a wall to stay out of the frantic traffic. "So, Molly, what brings you to Pelican Rapids?"

"I'm one of Mrs. Milton's mail-order brides from Georgia." If Mandy was from Pelican Rapids she'd know Mrs. Milton had brought several brides from the South.

Mandy nodded. "Yes, Mrs. Milton is famous for her brides. I didn't know there were any more eligible bachelors left. Who are you marrying?"

"Luke Ferrell. Do you know him?"

Mandy spewed her lemonade. Droplets hit Molly's bodice, making her step back.

A horrified look crossed Mandy's face. "Oh, I'm so sorry. Yes, I know Luke well. My mother thinks I'm coming home to marry him."

Now it was Molly's turn to drop her jaw. "What?"

Mandy shook her head, making the feather in her hat twirl crazily. "Not to worry. I'm engaged to another, though my mother doesn't know that. I've been visiting my grandparents in New York." She leaned in as though sharing a secret. "I went there to find a dentist to work on my teeth, and guess what, he fixed my teeth and asked me to marry him." She reared back, a satisfied look on her face. "That's why I'm coming home, to tell the folks."

"Why does your mother think you would marry Luke?"

Mandy threw her head back and let out an exaggerated sigh. "You'd have to know my mother to understand. She thinks if she wants something to be true, if she keeps saying it, it will come true."

When Molly scowled her sympathy, Mandy quickly added, "Oh, don't get me wrong. I love Mama, but she can be so...difficult. Thing is, I didn't even realize it until I got away from her and just in time, too. I'm not a spring chicken any more, and if I hadn't left Pelican Rapids, I would never have gotten married. I fear it's too late for my older sister, Jenny, and if my younger sister doesn't change her ways, she'll never catch a husband."

"Why don't they ask Mrs. Milton for help?" For that matter, why hadn't Mandy?

"Oh, Mama doesn't believe in selecting a mate through the mail. She'll look down her nose at you, my dear, but just ignore her."

Molly sipped her lemonade thoughtfully. "So, you never had feelings for Luke?"

"Oh, I admit I did at first. When he first arrived at his grandparents' farm, I went out to pick the eggs every day. He let us have them to sell in the store. But after several months, it became obvious he only thought of me as a friend. And I'm so thankful he did. If I'd married Luke, I would never have met Thomas.

"You'll love Luke, Molly. He's such a nice man, and handsome."

"He sent me a tin-type. Is his hair brown? It looked lighter than mine."

"Much lighter. In the summer it gets blond from the sun." Mandy laughed. "Luke is bad about forgetting his hat."

"What color are his eyes?"

Mandy twisted her mouth to the side. "That's a good question. His eyes seem to change color at times. They have some blue and green, maybe some brown too. I think you'd call it hazel." Mandy wagged her brows. "You'll like what you see. I hope I get to attend your wedding, but I'm only planning on staying a week. Do you know when your wedding day is?"

"No, Mrs. Milton will be making the arrangements, but I gathered she expected Luke and me to have some time to get acquainted." Molly hoped it wouldn't be delayed too long. She was eager to claim her husband and settle down in her own home.

"Yes, I think that's how it works." Mandy glanced over her shoulder, her head tipped, obviously checking the large train station clock.

"Actually, we have more in common than you realize," Molly said. "I left without my father's knowledge. He was opposed to this match, and I just hope he doesn't follow me." That was the first time such a thought entered her mind, but she wouldn't put it past him. "Although I'm hoping after he gets used to the idea, he'll come to the wedding."

"Oh, I hope he doesn't cause any trouble. Parents have a hard time realizing their children have grown up and can make decisions for themselves." Mandy took Molly's glass. "Here, I'll take these back and we'll be on our way. The trip to Pelican Rapids is a long one. We'll have plenty of time to discuss our troublesome parents, and I'll tell you all about Luke."

Chapter 6

These six things the Lord hates. Yes, seven are an abomination to Him: A proud look, a lying tongue, hands that shed blood, a heart that devises wicked plans, feet that are swift in running to evil, a false witness who speaks lies, and one who sows discord among brethren. – Proverbs 6:16-19

Dew still glistened on the grass when Luke charged

into town on Feckless, one of his roan work horses. He'd brought the pair from his parents' farm in Wisconsin where his pa managed a small herd of dairy cattle. He had broken Feckless and Reckless to the saddle as two-year-olds, and had trained them to respond with speed and agility.

Reckless's name to the contrary, he was as well trained as any in the West and would be a perfect mount for Molly. That brought to mind the reason for this early morning trek.

Molly was never far from his mind.

In his saddlebag, he carried the house plans he'd sketched the previous night.

He hoped the sawmill had enough lumber in stock. He'd worked at the sawmill when he'd first come to Pelican Rapids, and the mill owner, Mr. Jensen, had paid him in building supplies to erect the house. His father had drummed into his brain the necessary to avoid going into debt under all circumstances. Trouble was, it had taken all year to earn enough to repair the fences and barn, as well as build the new house. But he'd been proud of that accomplishment. He'd avoided having to put up the farm for a loan.

Now, here he was on his way to the bank to do just that.

Well, his father also said, a man had to do what he had to do for his family. When he'd decided to take a wife, Luke hadn't realized all he might have to do.

He slowed Feckless to a walk as he turned on Ash Street. A lady came out of the bank, making him pull in the reins. He'd always thought the bank opened later than this. Curtis Mills, the manager, was said to be the richest man in town, and that must mean he knew how to manage money. Luke needed advice and money.

Feckless snorted as Luke dismounted and searched the saddlebag. "Sorry, ole son, no grass to munch on here, but I shouldn't be long." He patted the horse's flank and tucked his papers under his arm.

The bank was empty of customers, but Mr. Mills sat at his desk behind the banister. He looked up when Luke closed the door. "Can I help you, Luke?"

Luke removed his hat. "I was thinking about taking out a loan."

"Come on, then. I'd be happy to discuss it with you." Mr. Mills held out a hand to the chair by his desk.

Luke came through the opening and lowered himself in the straight chair, one so hard it would be impossible to get comfortable in. He laid the sketch of his plans on the desk, along with materials list and estimated costs. "I need to build onto my house, and this is the amount I figure it'll cost." He pointed to the total.

Mr. Mills's smile disappeared. "I see. How's the farm doing this year? I see you have a good stand of corn, but predictions are for lower corn prices."

Luke cleared his throat. He hated talking about the farm. Truth was, it was still in poor shape. He hadn't been able to get enough acreage cleared to plant a full crop of anything. "I have some alfalfa."

"Livestock feed doesn't bring much. You'd do better with wheat."

Luke coughed. "Yes sir, the farm would make more in wheat, but I've a mind to start a dairy and make cheese. I brought my folks' old equipment and the grandfolks' old soddy will make a good place for the cheese to ripen."

The smile returned. "A dairy farm you say. We don't have one in the area, and cheese would be a good money-making venture. How many cows do you have?"

Luke tried to find a more comfortable position. "Well, I'll need to borrow money for that too. I've a mind to add three or four Jerseys by winter and double the number each year so I'll have enough in four years to support the farm." And a family, he hoped.

Mr. Mills shook his head. "I'm sorry, but I don't see that you'll have enough income for a loan of this size."

"I'll be putting up the land. It's worth more than

that."

"That's true, Luke, but this bank isn't in the business of taking a man's land. We want customers who are able to pay loans off from their income."

"But if it's a risk I'm willing to take, I'd think the bank could go along with it. You see, Mr. Mills, I'm getting married, and I need to provide my wife with a decent place to live."

Mr. Mills slapped the desktop. "That's right. I heard you're getting married to one of the Carter daughters. Well, that's your answer. I'm sure Mr. Carter will lend you the money to make a more comfortable home for his daughter. He might be willing to give you the money."

Oh no. Luke drew in a lungful of air. He'd thought he'd squashed those rumors. "I'm not getting married to Mandy Carter, or any of the Carter daughters. My wife-to-be is coming from Georgia. It was arranged by Mrs. Milton's agency."

Mr. Mills reared back like Luke had slapped him. "A mail-order bride?" He seemed to realize his tone was derogatory, and his tone turned conciliatory. Almost downright condescending. "Don't get me wrong. Those ladies Mrs. Milton brings in are lovely, but they have nothing to bring to the marriage—except themselves."

"That's all I ask of my wife."

"Yes...sorry. I didn't mean to offend, but I'd heard you were to marry Mandy Carter. Let me jot down these figures. I'll discuss it with the board and let you know how much we can loan you. How's that?"

"When will I have an answer?"

"By next week."

Luke got to his feet. "Fair enough. Thank you, Mr. Mills." He shook the banker's hand and took his leave. Next stop, the mercantile, to stop Mrs. Carter's stupid rumor once and for all.

He stuffed his papers back in the saddlebag and mounted Feckless. A short distance, he crossed the Pelican River and turned straight up Main Street to the Mercantile.

Fortunately, the store was void of customers, but Mrs. Carter was standing at the fabric table, straightening bolts of calico. As soon as the little bell heralded his entrance, she looked up, a wide smile on her plump face. "Hello, Luke. What brings you back to town? Did you forget something the other day?"

He didn't bother to remove his hat. "I stopped at the bank. Mrs. Carter, you have to stop telling people Mandy and I are getting hitched."

She laughed. "It's just a matter of time. I've seen you two together. Remember the spring picnic? You two went off by yourselves." She peered at him slyly from under her lashes.

He'd rescued Mandy from her family at her request. That was all. "I enjoy Mandy's company. We're friends, but that's all there is to it. And I'm getting married to a lady from Georgia as I told you before, but I'm telling you again in case you didn't hear me."

"Oh, I've heard all right. But you haven't even met this woman. You know nothing about her except what Ella Milton has told you."

It was a good thing they weren't near a wall. He would be tempted to put his head through it. "I've received four letters from Molly herself. I know she's the one I want to marry."

Mrs. Carter kept smiling as she nodded. "Words written on paper. How do you know if any of it is true?" She hiked her nose in the air. "This mail-order bride is supposed to come in next week, I hear. Mandy is already on the train and will be arriving Friday at noon."

Luke groaned. "That's when Molly is scheduled to arrive."

"How interesting that will be. Did you know Mandy got her teeth fixed? When the mister and I went to visit his parents last month we couldn't believe the transformation in our Mandy. She has such a beautiful smile. And Grandma Carter took her to buy a new wardrobe, including a wedding gown."

"That's nice. Did you meet the man she wants to marry?"

Mrs. Carter chuckled and slapped at his sleeve. "She's just trying to make you jealous writing about her beau. There is no beau. You mark my words, you and Mandy will be married before the summer's over."

It was useless to argue. "Good-day to you, Mrs. Carter." He turned on his heel.

She followed him to the door. "As soon as you meet this mail-order bride, you'll find she's not what you've pictured in your mind, and you'll come to your senses. And it might be you won't be what she expected. She might get back on the train and leave."

He didn't look back. "That was a total waste of time, Feckless," he told the horse. Feckless whinnied like he understood. Maybe Mrs. Carter was right. What if Molly took one look at him and decided he wasn't the man she'd pictured?

He slammed the door shut to that thought. Molly wasn't a fickle woman. She was as committed to this marriage as he was. Besides, she couldn't just up and return to Georgia. She'd sent him her piano.

Keeping Feckless at a walk to accommodate the increasing traffic, Luke continued on Main all the way to Birch. He heard the rapids before they came into view. His senses always came alive at this spot.

The rushing water brought to mind the Scripture in Revelation about the sound of many waters at the throne of God. There was a sense of movement and peace. Power. Life. Music. As he entered the sawmill area, the music of the rapids blended with the saws in a medley of highs and lows. A humming followed by a crash in a never-ending ebb and flow.

The feel of this place was just as refreshing. Even in the hottest part of summer, the temperature dropped the closer one got to the water. It never failed that Feckless wanted to stop and drink, but Luke urged him to the hitching post and tethered him securely.

He retrieved his building plans and stopped beside the giant water wheel, splashing its own notes to the orchestra. He breathed in the smell of freshly cut wood, a fragrance that demanded time to be savored.

Luke had known Dag Jensen, the mill operator, since he'd worked at the mill in return for the lumber to build his house. That's why he hadn't had the time to cultivate more farmland. There was only so much time in the day.

Mr. Jensen came from the back yard. He was a tall, muscular Viking-type of around fifty with a shock of silver blond hair, piercing blue eyes, and a ready smile. A true lumberjack.

Luke liked the man for a lot of reasons, mostly

because, for all his hulk, he was one of the gentlest fellows around town. "You looking for a job, Luke." Mr. Jensen held out a beefy hand, his red plaid shirt sleeves rolled up to reveal trunk-sized, silver-haired arms.

A job? That hadn't crossed Luke's mind, but now that it did— "I might, for a fact. You need help?"

"Do I ever? I let my son go off on a Canadian buying trip, and had to fire that last fellow. Came in drunk twice." Mr. Jensen held out two fat fingers.

"That's too bad."

"Dangerous. You know you have to have your wits about you operating the saws—or you'll wish you had."

True. Luke had come close to getting sliced a couple of times. That was enough to sober him, even if he was still a drinking man, which he wasn't.

"Well, to tell the truth, I think I can spare the time. I've been trying to plow another field for next year's planting, but this year's corn is growing without my help. Maybe we can work out a deal like before." He pulled his building list from his pocket and unfolded it.

"I'm building another room and need this much lumber. If I could work it off, do you have enough in stock?" He held his breath. This could save him from having to take out a loan, and that would make for a more pleasant winter for him and Molly.

"Ja, I have enough pine already cured."

Pine wouldn't last as long as cedar or redwood, but if it was painted each year, it would hold out. "That would be fine with me."

Mr. Jensen nodded. "You can give me six weeks—until my son returns?"

Luke would rather spend time with Molly, but hopefully, she'd understand. He jutted his hand at the mill owner. "It's a deal."

They shook hands. "I'd like to start tomorrow. I'll bring the buckboard and take the lumber back after work." He knew they wouldn't quit until after sunset.

"You could start today," Jensen said.

"I have some more business to tend to today, but I'll be in at daybreak tomorrow."

Reluctantly, he left the pleasant sights and sounds of the sawmill and the rapids. He untied Feckless's reins and ran a hand down the horse's neck. "It just goes to show you." He swung into the saddle. "Like the Lord says, worry is wasted time." The horse turned his head, his ears twitched. Luke would swear the horse listened to every word he said.

Being alone did that to him—got him in the

habit of talking to the animals. Almost expecting them to answer back.

Soon he'd have Molly to talk to. Everything was going to work out. Now all he'd have to do was find the time to do chores at the farm, build Molly's music room, and give Mr. Jensen an honest day's work for the next six weeks.

Chapter 7

I was a stranger, and ye took me in. Matthew 25:35

With a belch of steam, a whistle blast, and the clacking of gears, the train pulled out of Chicago. The passenger car was filled to capacity, and a few men standing in the aisle. The noise of conversation, babies crying, and the conductor's instructions made it difficult to hear each other, but Molly and Mandy found a seat together.

As the noise level lowered Mandy kept up non-stop chatter. Molly was a good listener, never having learned how to interject her thoughts while another was talking. But she was bursting with questions. This was the last leg of her journey. In mere hours, she'd be in Minnesota, then Pelican Rapids—her new home. Mandy lived there so she could prepare her for what to expect.

Mandy wanted to talk about nothing but Thomas. She was deeply in love, but she had cared for Luke at one time and must know him well. If only Molly could steer the conversation to him. Would she come to love Luke as much as Mandy loved Thomas? Would Luke love her?

Strange, she hadn't even thought to question that. People who got married would love each other. Wouldn't they? "How did you first know that Thomas loved you?" she finally blurted in the middle of Mandy's sentence. "I mean, did you think that might happen when you first met him?"

Mandy laughed. "Goodness, no. I dreaded going to his office. Afraid of how much pain I'd have to go through, you know." She pushed back against the cushions. "But he was so kind and gentle." She giggled again. "And handsome. Even from the first meeting, we talked about everything. Things I'd never have said to another man." She drew in a breath. "There's nothing like love. Are you nervous about meeting Luke?"

"Yes, very. The closer we get the more butterflies beat in my stomach."

A look of sympathy showed in Mandy's eyes. "Luke is very sweet. You will love him from the first."

But would he love her? Surely it would take time for both of them, but there was no time. Mrs. Milton expected them to get married within weeks, and Molly didn't want to wait that long. "Tell me about Pelican Rapids? Does it have rapids?"

"Oh, yes, right in the center of town, and the river runs swiftly all the time."

Molly smiled. There were lots of rapids around Juliette, though they were hidden in the woods. Still, this would be something familiar to her. "I wish you were staying in town longer. I'll miss you."

Mandy patted her knee. "Within a week, you'll have lots of lady friends. Mrs. Milton will make sure of that, and everyone will be excited about your wedding. It depends on what kind of reception I get from my family as to whether I can stay longer than a week."

"But surely they'll accept your decision after you tell them about Thomas and how much you love each other."

"Mama says he's too old for me" She lowered her

voice. "He's thirty-two and I'm twenty-two."

"That's not so much. I knew a couple who were thirty years apart in age, and they seemed very happy."

Mandy dropped her gaze to her lap. "I don't feel it matters, but my mother gets her mind set about something and she won't let go."

Was that Daddy's problem too? He was so set in his ways he'd never accept a Yankee son-in-law. He couldn't let go of the war and all the devastation left in its wake. Molly bit the inside of her cheek and pondered that as the countryside sped by her window.

"If all goes well, I'm going to send word for Thomas to come get me. I just pray my folks treat him civilly. I might have to send him a telegram and tell him I'll return alone."

"So you're getting married in New York?"

"Yes, my grandparents can't travel, and they are paying for the wedding. Grandma says Mama and Papa can travel better than they can. She's as outspoken as Mama." Mandy giggled again. "Grandfather is paying for our honeymoon to Niagara Falls. Talk about rapids."

Molly knew there wouldn't be a honeymoon for her and Luke, but she hoped Daddy would come to the wedding. She'd always imagined walking down the aisle on Daddy's arm. "I suppose you'll have a big wedding." It sounded like Mandy's grandparents were well-to-do.

"Yes, it's going to be in the garden. I don't have the exact date yet, because Grandma is clearing the schedule with her friends, but it will be sometime in August. If it's at all possible, we'd love for you and Luke to attend."

"I'd love to come, but I doubt Luke can leave the farm during the summer." Or spring. Or fall.

"That's one of the drawbacks to farming, I guess. You're bound to the land."

Molly nodded. That was true unless you had others working the land for you. Like Daddy had before the war. They used to go to the Georgia coast during summer, visiting her aunt and uncle. Such fun she'd had playing with her cousins. She didn't know if they were still living. The war had torn families apart.

"Does Thomas have his own house?"

"He lives in an apartment now, but he's searching for our house, and when I return, we'll find one together. He says I must approve because it will be my domain." She bounded to the edge of her seat. "Did I mention that Luke has built you a house? It's a very nice farmhouse."

"I can't wait to see it." Her own home. Thankfully, she had experience in keeping house for Daddy. She could cook and clean, garden, and sew. She could milk and take care of the livestock and chickens. Everything except kill the chickens. She hoped Luke would do that for her.

That set Mandy off into another litany of Thomas's plans for them. Molly listened politely, and she could understand Mandy's exuberance, but she would rather have heard about Luke.

Eventually, Mandy wore out Thomas's virtues and quieted. The whole train grew quieter as children settled and their mothers read or did needlework. Many of the men gathered in another car to discuss politics and business and whatever else men talked about.

She wished the window wasn't darkened with soot. It would be nice to clearly see this land she was moving to. Her fingers worked under the hem of her sleeve until she found the handkerchief hidden there. She blotted the moisture on her brow. The air hadn't cooled much during the night. Wasn't the North supposed to be cooler than the South? But to be fair, the press of bodies inside this train car added to the heat.

Mandy had fallen asleep. Molly didn't blame her. Both of them had been so excited last night, neither had slept much. Sleep still evaded her, so she clasped her hands together in prayer. *Lord, prepare Luke's and my hearts to love each other. Show me how to be the type of wife he desires. And if it wouldn't be too much trouble, please send me peace so I don't act like a fool.*

She petitioned God with all her fears, one after another, until her eyelids grew heavy.

The screeching of train brakes jolted Molly awake. She looked out the window and billowing steam obscured what little she could see through the grime. They must have arrived at Pelican Rapids, and she'd slept through the conductor's announcement.

She swung her gaze to the left and found Mandy missing. Mild panic rose in her chest, although her brain told her Mandy couldn't possibly have gotten off the train without her.

This wasn't a mere water stop. Passengers were standing, shouting orders to each other and retrieving their bags from overhead and under the seats.

"I'm here," Mandy called from behind a tall man trying to gather his family together. As soon as the man got out of the way, she held back to allow Molly to enter the flow of people anxious to set feet on solid ground. Mandy pulled her carpetbag with her. "I had to go to the necessary and didn't have the heart to wake you."

"I wish you had. I must look a mess." She'd changed into a clean dress this morning, a difficult feat in the small lavatory, but it was now as wrinkled as before. Hopefully, Luke would understand.

"You look beautiful," Mandy said. "Here, hold your hat while I reset these pins."

As they shuffled down the aisle, Molly felt her new friend poking through her hair, and then, resettling the blue flower bedecked hat on her head. She sent a smile over her shoulder. "Thank you."

Mandy gave both her shoulders a squeeze. "Everything will be fine. All of Mrs. Milton's brides have been warmly welcomed, and you will too."

Molly knew she wasn't in Georgia anymore as soon as she stepped onto the wooden depot platform. A gentle breeze caressed her face with pleasant air—not cool, but not hot either, though the sun was high in the cloudless sky. Just right.

A small crowd waited as the passengers disembarked. Shouts of recognition and welcome filled the air. Two women bounded forward, waving both hands. "That's Mama and my sister, Jenny," Mandy said from close behind. She waved and rushed forward.

Most of the passengers left immediately, and the crowd thinned. Molly searched the street for Luke. She couldn't find any man that would match his description. But Mandy gestured to her.

"Mama, Jenny, this is Molly Stewart, our newest mail-order bride."

"Welcome to Pelican Rapids, Miss Stewart."

Mrs. Carter's smile didn't fit her narrowed gaze, but maybe she was squinting against the glaring sunlight.

"Pleased to meet you both." She lifted her eyes to scan the other side of the street. "Where is Luke?"

Mandy sent a worried look that way. "Yes, where is Luke? Didn't he know when Molly's train would arrive?"

"I expect he's busy. It's the middle of the day, after all."

Too busy to meet her. Molly forced her lips into the shape of a smile.

"We'll take you to Ella Milton's place," Mrs. Carter said. "She's expecting you."

Mandy's exuberance returned. She grabbed Molly on one side and her sister on the other and made a beeline for a waiting buggy. They waited for Mrs. Carter, who was greeting some other lady. Mandy whispered in Molly's ear. "I know Luke must have a good reason for not meeting you." She jerked back, her eyes popping. "I'll bet he's at Mrs. Milton's house, just waiting for you."

Chapter 8

Wealth makes many friends. But the poor is separated from his friend. -Proverbs 19:4

Over the roar of the giant saw, Luke thought he heard the train whistle. Startled, he jerked, almost losing grip of the eighteen-inch log he was feeding into the saw. It couldn't be that late. He'd asked

Johnny to tell him when one-thirty arrived, a half-hour before the train was due in. But apparently, Johnny forgot. There was nothing Luke could do now but let the saw finish its work. If he ruined a high-quality oak log, he'd lose a week's pay.

As soon as the log cleared, he turned off the machine. "Johnny, get out here."

The teenager came sauntering from the office building, not a sign of any concern.

"Why didn't you come tell me when it was one-thirty? I told you I had to meet the train."

"Is it one-thirty already? We had a string of customers I had to take care of."

Yeah, Luke knew how he took care of customers, chewing the fat for as long as they'd listen. "Never mind. I'll be back as soon as I can, but tell Mr. Jensen I'll finish up this oak before I go home. He knows I have to meet someone from the train."

A grin spread across Johnny's freckled face. "Your mail-order bride?"

Luke frowned. That news was all over town by now. "I hope she'll still be willing to be my bride after this." He shed his leather apron and rushed to the pump. Dousing his head under the water, he washed his hair and face. After drying off, he brushed as much sawdust as possible off his shirt and trousers. He'd worn his Sunday best, but that was a mistake. The white shirt was sweat drenched

68

and the black trousers speckled with sawdust.

Nothing he could do about that now. He slammed the bowler on his still wet head. He looked like the farmer he was. Nothing he could do about that either.

He mounted Feckless in a fluid motion and took off toward Mrs. Milton's, leaving a trail of dust in his wake. As he rounded Main onto Plum, Tillie Johnston ran out in front of him, hands waving. He had to pull in sharply to avoid plowing into her.

Feckless pawed the air, but Tillie looked unfazed by her near fatal accident. "Luke," she spurted between heaving breaths. "Could you split me some wood? I just realized I'm completely out and I have a lot of cooking to do for tomorrow's church meeting."

Luke shoved back in the saddle, everything in him wanting to tip his hat to sweet but crazy Miz Tillie and be on his way. "I'm late to meet somebody, Miz Tillie, but—"

"I'll be making two chocolate cakes for the church picnic that's to welcome your bride. I know how much you like them. Mrs. Milton gave me the cocoa and sugar, special."

Why was he arguing? By the time she got through explaining he could have the wood split. He swung down and walked beside her to her house. "What picnic?"

"You weren't at church last Sunday when it was announced," Miz Tillie said, a mild scolding flavoring her words.

He'd overslept last Sunday because he'd plowed the fields until past midnight. Too much to do and too little time. He thought the Lord would understand, but he wouldn't take time to explain to Miz Tillie. "How much wood will it take to do your baking?"

Miz Tillie walked on ahead of him. "I don't know. Just fill the wood box," she said over her shoulder. "Oh, and don't forget the kindling."

Fill the wood box? That would take a cord of wood for her wood box. He knew because he'd built it on her rickety back porch so she'd have enough to carry her through a blizzard.

There wasn't a blizzard in sight so she'd have to make do with a wheelbarrow full today. He split the logs into stove sized sticks and picked up a few handfuls of splinters for kindling. After dropping it all off in the wood box, he got back underway.

As he was rounding the house, he spied a yellow rose bush. The blooms were about as pretty as he'd ever seen. He could tell from her letters, Molly loved flowers. "Miz Tillie," he yelled, "may I cut a few of your roses?"

Her muffled voice carried from within the house. "Help yourself, Luke."

He selected twelve of the best, some just budding, some full-blown. Tillie's front door screeched open, and the spry little lady came out. "Here, Luke, something to tie them together. I couldn't find a ribbon."

"Thank you, ma'am." He took the frayed short length of rope from her outstretched hand and bound the roses together. The make-shift tie looked surprisingly nice.

"They're right pretty this year," Miz Tillie said. "Perfect for a beautiful lady—and she's really beautiful, Luke. Pretty don't even come close."

"You've met Molly...er...Miss Stewart?"

"No, but I saw her down at the depot. I wanted to welcome her to town, but Theodora Carter took over and I couldn't get close. They loaded onto the Carter buggy and hightailed it to Mrs. Milton's place."

Luke groaned inwardly. This wasn't what he needed.

"Theodora's daughter, Mandy, came in off the train with Molly," Miz Tillie continued.

Pent up tension seeped out of Luke as he considered that. The situation wasn't as bad as he thought. Mandy would be able to explain about her mother to Molly. "Thank you again for the flowers, Miz Tillie." He waved and climbed into the saddle.

Feckless had hardly worked up a canter before

Luke stopped in front of Ella Milton's house. With the roses in one hand, he ran his other down the horse's side, taking a moment to gather his nerves.

His knock on the door was answered almost immediately by Mrs. Milton herself. She gave him a welcoming smile. "Come in, Luke." Her gaze slid to the bouquet. "You didn't have to bring me flowers."

He cleared his throat. "I...uh—"

She laughed. "I was teasing. I know who they're for. Oh, Minnie, would you fill a vase with water for Molly's roses. We'll set it in the parlor by the burgundy sofa." She turned to Luke. "Go on in and make yourself comfortable. I'll get Molly."

It had been years since Luke had courted a lady, but all those memories and nerves came rushing back as he sat on the deep red sofa in the parlor, with the roses balanced on his knees. He didn't have to wait long. Mrs. Milton returned, followed by the most beautiful woman he'd ever seen.

He shot to his feet. Now he knew what the poets meant by a magnolia complexion. Creamy with pink-tinged cheeks. Her full rosy lips spread in a heart-stopping smile. From under sweeping lashes, she gazed at him with dark, smoldering eyes.

"I'm so pleased to finally meet you, Luke." Her voice, soft and sweet, almost done him in.

Bemused, he stupidly shoved the roses into her outstretched hand.

"Thank you, Luke...I mean...Mr. Ferrell." She blushed, making her face even prettier. "I've been thinking of you by your first name for the longest time."

She had? "That's all right. I've been thinking of you as nothing but Molly." And that was all the time.

Having ducked her head, she glanced up, favoring him with a lovely smile. "The flowers are so thoughtful and beautiful. No one has ever given me yellow roses, and they're my favorite." She stared at the flowers for several seconds, and when she looked up again, he could swear tears filmed her eyes.

He swallowed the lump in his throat. "I'm sure glad about that. I figured since you liked yellow houses, you'd like yellow roses." What a stupid thing to say. He rushed on, breathlessly, "I'm sorry I wasn't at the depot to meet the train, but I got delayed."

"I understand, but don't be sorry. It gave me a chance to freshen up a bit in the beautiful room Mrs. Milton gave me."

"Please, have a seat." The lady herself came into the room. "I don't know what's taking Minnie so long. Just give me those lovely roses, Molly, and I'll put them in water," Mrs. Milton said.

Luke waited until Molly had relinquished the flowers and settled on the sofa before dropping beside her, keeping a respectful distance between them, but close enough to get a whiff of her perfume that reminded him of lilacs.

Mrs. Milton stood, smiling like she was mighty pleased. "Minnie will have dinner on the table in a few moments. What would you folks like to drink with your meal? Tea, coffee, or water?"

"Tea, if you please," Molly said, "with a heaping spoonful of sugar."

Stood to reason such a sweet lady would like sweet things. Luke tucked that bit of information to the back of his mind. "Could you make mine coffee—black?" He needed something strong to wake up his brain.

He heard Mrs. Milton's skirts swish as she left them, then silence fell and both he and Molly scanned the well-appointed room. Looking everywhere except at each other.

Think of something to say, he admonished himself, but she broke the silence first. "Did my piano arrive?"

He found that dark chocolate gaze on him and turned sideways. "Yes, I got it set up at the house."

"You had enough room for it, I hope. It's so large, I worried about that."

He caught the chuckle that rose in his throat in

time. "There's room." Or there would be before they were married. "It's a beautiful piano. I can understand why you wanted to bring it."

"It's the only thing I have left of my mother's, and she loved it so. When may I see the house?"

He coughed into his fist. "I'd like you to wait until after the wedding. Truth is, Molly, there's work still to finish on the house."

He could tell she wasn't pleased with that answer when her brows wrinkled, and it looked like she had trouble lifting those rosy lips into a smile. "Then maybe you can show me the town and some of the countryside."

Now he frowned. When was he going to find the time to squire her around town? He was promised at the sawmill half days and that meant he had to work the fields at night while there was enough moonlight. He'd just have to find some time. "I'd enjoy that. Do you ride?"

"Oh, yes, I can ride a horse. I've been riding since I was a little girl. I even have a riding habit with a split skirt. I hope that isn't taboo up here."

He honestly didn't know what was considered taboo in women's dress. "I imagine if it was all right in Georgia, it'll be all right here. But Mrs. Milton might have a sidesaddle."

"Maybe I should use the sidesaddle, then. Riding astride is frowned upon by the city ladies, but us country women, after the war, had to cover greater distances any way we could."

His fear that she was too fancy for the farming life went down several notches. But he didn't want to steer clear of anything having to do with the war.

He told her about the mount he had in mind for her and felt his taunt muscles relax when she leaned toward him, an eager spark in those dark eyes. He delighted in her musical laughter as he described Feckless's and Reckless's antics.

Mrs. Milton returned, carrying a vase holding the yellow roses. Her cook, Minnie, tagged along behind, probably to get a good gander at the two of them together before announcing dinner.

Luke slid back against the sofa's cushions. His and Molly's time of intimacy was over for now. Mrs. Milton would be joining them. But there would be other times, busy or not, he'd make sure of it.

Chapter 9

A man has joy by the answer of his mouth, and a word spoken in due season, how good it is! Proverbs 15:23

Molly couldn't miss that Luke was nervous. Truth to tell, her own stomach was trying to tie itself in knots. The food looked delicious. Braised pork chops smothered in a rich gravy, fluffy white potatoes, stewed pole beans, summer squash and scallions. She simply couldn't do any of it justice.

"Luke, dear, would you bless the food tonight?"

"I'd be pleased to ma'am." He offered his left hand to Mrs. Milton, who sat at the end of the table, and Molly to his right. His touch warmed her all the way to her center.

"Gracious Father God, we thank you for this feast prepared with loving hands, and ask Your blessings on all our friends and neighbors present or missing. Thank You for bringing Molly into our midst...and...help us carry out Your will in our lives."

What a sweet and heart-felt prayer. Molly sent her own thanksgiving heavenward for bringing her to this man.

When the last amen sounded, Minnie waved her hand. "Well, folks, dig in."

Fearing her lack of appetite might insult Minnie, she slowly partook of all, while Mrs. Milton and Minnie kept up a banter with Mrs. Milton's son, Josiah, about some town event that meant nothing to Molly at the moment.

She kept an eye on Luke out of the corner of her eye. He sure had a good appetite and as soon as he'd emptied his plate, Minnie was at his side refilling it like she was used to hungry men. Josiah, too, asked for seconds. But why not. These men worked in the fields all day. It would take a lot to keep them filled.

Molly suspected she'd have to bake a dozen biscuits at the time for her new husband. She couldn't compete with Minnie's cooking, but she could make a decent biscuit.

Lost in future plans and having nothing to contribute to the conversation, she picked at her food. Luke's gaze finally landed on her. She dipped her head and studied the blue willow pattern in her dinner plate like it was the most fascinating thing she'd ever seen.

She shouldn't be so bashful around Luke. In her mind's eye, she'd played out dozens of teasing, flirtatious things to say to him. She'd never been nervous around men before. But this was the first one she'd ever intended to marry. To kiss. To live with. To care for.

"Have you two set a date for the wedding?" Mrs. Milton asked.

Molly's head jerked up to meet Luke's gaze over the rim of his coffee cup. They stared at each other for a little too long, and Mrs. Milton added, "There's no hurry on my part, but several of the ladies would like to get started on wedding plans."

Luke set his cup down. "I should have our house ready by the middle of July."

"But that's too late." Minnie reared back in her chair. "We'll have a lot of people in for the Fourth of July celebration, and they'll want to attend the wedding."

"Minnie, Luke may not have even known about our guests. Did you tell him, Molly?"

"Tell him?" She didn't know about them either.

"Yes, dear. Remember I mentioned in my letter that my Southern brides and their families wanted to give you and Luke a big wedding and reception, and since it was so close to the Independence Day celebration, many of our friends would be in town. You're my fifth bride from the South."

Molly did recall the letter, but she'd thought of it as a it-would-be-nice thing, not a we're-counting-on-it thing. "Eh, yes, I do, and I'm so honored that everyone wants to participate in our wedding. I was just taken aback for a moment. I hadn't anticipated a big wedding. I don't even have a...that is, I'll have to fix my wedding gown."

"Don't worry about that." Minnie offered Luke some more coffee, which he waved off. "The ladies' sewing circle will be happy to sew a beautiful wedding gown."

Molly sent a fleeting glance to Luke who looked like he'd lost his appetite. "Don't you agree, Luke? I would like a church wedding."

He smiled. "Then we'll have a church wedding." Inclining his head in Mrs. Milton's direction, he added, "We'll leave the wedding preparations in your capable hands, Miz Ella, just make it as close to the Fourth of July as possible and get Reverend Lawrence's agreement."

"Oh, he knows. He's just waiting for a date to put on his calendar. And Grace is on the wedding committee."

Molly looked a question to Luke. "Grace?" she whispered.

"Reverend Lawrence's wife."

"Dinner was delicious, Minnie, and I'll bid you all good-evening. I have to see to the stock." Josiah stood and helped his mother to her feet, signaling the end of the meal.

Luke did the same for Molly. "Thank you, ladies, for inviting me to dinner. It was the best I've eaten in some time."

"Glad you enjoyed it." Minnie was already up and gathering the dishes.

"Can I help you clean up?" Molly asked.

"Goodness no, child." Minnie waved her off with a dishcloth. "You're a guest. Just give us leave to make your wedding the best."

Guest or not, every Southern woman offered to help her host, at least after the war when most of them had lost their kitchen help.

Mrs. Milton came up between Molly and Luke. "Now, you two don't pay any attention to Minnie.

Go into the parlor and discuss your wedding plans, and we'll make the arrangements however you wish."

Luke offered his arm and Molly took it readily. They did have much to discuss.

But when they'd settled on the burgundy-colored sofa, both seemed reluctant to start the conversation. Molly wasn't surprised to find Luke quiet. His letters had been short. Sweet, but short. Some men, maybe all men, were like that. But what was wrong with her? Ever since she'd first decided to marry Luke, she'd been gathering up all the things she wanted to say to him. To ask him. Now her brain froze.

Then the enormity of the situation suddenly hit her. She would soon be wedded to this man who was still a stranger. Wedded. Husband and wife. Living together. Till death.

He kept yawning, which meant he was tired. Or bored.

Sure, he was bored. She was sitting here like a bump on a log. Mama used to say it was up to the lady to interest the gentleman. What did he enjoy doing, other than farming?

She found inspiration from the bookshelf. He did like to read—adventure, if she remembered correctly. Darting to the tall bookshelf, she searched for the book she'd noticed earlier. "Have you read Jules Verne?"

"Yes, I've read *Journey to the Center of the Earth*. It's rather fantastic. Don't tell me you've read it."

She returned to the sofa with book in hand. "No, but this is Mr. Verne's latest tome, *Twenty Thousand Leagues under the Sea.*"

Luke twisted to face her, his knee brushing her dress. "Molly, I don't want you to think I was trying to put our wedding off. Truth is, tomorrow wouldn't be too soon for me."

The book fell into her lap. "It wouldn't?"

He reached out his hand and touched her cheek. "I'm more than ready. I've been thinking of nothing else since I got your first letter, and when I first saw you...well, it kind of knocked the breath out of me, and I couldn't believe a beautiful woman like you would marry me."

His words knocked the breath right out of her, too. She just stared, hoping he'd kiss her and afraid if he did, she might faint.

His hand went to his mouth as he stifled another yawn, and she regained her senses. "That's very sweet of you to say, Luke, but I suppose we must give Mrs. Milton and her brides a big wedding."

"If that's your wish. Would you mind reading to me? I love listening to your voice. It has a soft, musical cadence as lovely as any song. Do you sing?"

Heat rose in her cheeks at the unexpected compliment. "Thank you. I sing a little as I play the piano, but I'd love to read for you. Shall I start with Mr. Verne?"

"Please." He stretched his long legs out and rested his head against the chair's cushion.

Molly smiled. She'd often read for Daddy before retiring for the night and took special care to add expression to the words. As she came to the end of the chapter, she'd become interested in the story. "I wonder how far twenty thousand leagues is."

When Luke didn't answer, she asked, "Do you know, Luke?" Marking her place, she swiveled her gaze his way.

Luke was asleep. He *was* tired. Sympathy welled within her. She knew how hard farmers worked at this time of year.

She started to wake him, then stilled her hand. He'd be embarrassed to be caught asleep. She slipped off the sofa, taking care not to disturb him, and strode to the bookshelf. Holding the book in front of her, she let it fall to the wooden floor with a crash.

As she'd hoped, the noise woke Luke and he was immediately at her side. She gave him a sly glance. "I'm so clumsy."

He plucked the book from the floor and she took it. "Luke, if you don't mind, I am rather fatigued tonight." She slid the book back in its place. "Can we continue the search for Captain Nemo another time?"

"Certainly, Molly. I should be getting along anyway. Chores are waiting."

She laid her hand on his arm. "Do you have much to do?"

"I have the stock to take care of, and if there's enough moonlight tonight, I'd like to get in a little harrowing."

Goodness. The poor man needed to go straight to bed. After they were married, she'd help him with the stock, and if he'd show her what to do, she'd help with the harrowing too. Whatever that was.

She handed him his hat at the door. "Will I see you at church tomorrow?"

His face lit up. "Tomorrow is Sunday, isn't it? Yes, I'll be there." He stood worrying his hat for several moments. "I can show you the town and countryside tomorrow afternoon."

She smiled. "I'd like that."

"Good-night, Molly." He took her hand and lifted it like he might kiss it, then leaned in and brushed her cheek with a fleeting kiss instead.

Surprised, her chin dropped, and the door closed behind him before she could shut her mouth. She touched her cheek and sent up a prayer for good weather tomorrow.

Chapter 10

My beloved spoke and said to me, "Rise up, my love, my fair one, and come away." Song of Solomon 2:10

Luke waited for Molly to adjust her seating on Feckless. He honestly didn't know how a lady could keep herself seated on the contraption called a sidesaddle, but Molly looked like she knew what she was doing—and very pretty doing it.

Not too many women rode horses in Pelican Rapids, and it had taken Jim Bailey, the ostler, an hour to find this sidesaddle buried in a pile of old harnesses. Luke offered to buy it, but Jim told him to take it. It had been lying there for years, and Jim recommended Luke grease the leather good or it would crack. That was mighty nice of him, and Luke promised to bring Mrs. Bailey a bushel of sweet corn when it was ready to pull.

When he was sure Molly was ready, he swung onto Reckless's back, and pulled up beside Feckless. "This little stretch is called Plum Lane, and it'll take us to town." He pointed to the dirt path unnecessarily.

Molly drew in a deep breath. "I love the smell of a farm. Everything blooming and growing." She swiveled her head toward the fields and drew in another exaggerated breath. "I can't wait to see ours."

Regret he didn't have as nice a place as this tightened his throat, and he rubbed his neck. "Well, it's not near as big or as well maintained as this one. Miz Ella's corn is a foot higher than mine."

She shifted her gaze back to him and favored him with a wide smile. "I'm sure it will catch up, and will produce more each year. Can we ride to the river then? I'd like to see the rapids, too."

"If you like, we can get to town that way." He nudged Reckless toward the woods and they took off. At the end of the drive, Molly surged ahead, and Luke had to slap Reckless's flank to catch up.

She looked over her shoulder, laughing, then slowed Feckless to a smooth gallop. "It's been so long since I've had a good ride."

"I thought you might be running away." He grinned, enjoying her playful mood. Living with Molly was going to be unpredictable, but fun.

"No, I'd never do that." She stretched in the saddle, her head tilted toward the sky, giving him a lovely view of her profile. With a slanted glance, she sent him a mischievous wink. "Besides, I don't know the town well enough to know where to go. As much as I'd like to race you to the river, I'd better take it slower. I'm sure to be sore tomorrow."

"You sit a horse very well. Confident. Old Feckless is cantankerous, but a horse can judge a rider who's boss."

"I lost my favorite horse in the war, a beautiful black thoroughbred named Starlight because he had a star marking on his muzzle. Daddy let Willian, my brother take him and neither returned."

He wished she hadn't mentioned the war. It brought back memories he'd rather stay buried. But he knew it impacted her more than him. She had to live with the aftermath, whereas he escaped back home. "I'm sorry for all you lost. It must have been devastating to everyone."

"I wrote about William, who was killed at the beginning of the war, and Mama who died that last year. Overall, our town wasn't affected much until the last. I mean there were those who lost men in battle, but somehow life went on. Maybe it wouldn't have been so shocking if I hadn't been sent south as the war was advancing."

"Where did you go?"

"Not far. I stayed with my aunt in Macon. Even there we heard cannon fire, but no soldiers came that far."

He wanted to know more about her. She hadn't written much about her earlier life. "Before the war life must have been much happier. Did your plantation house have a name?"

"Yes, it was called the White House, though it wasn't as big as the one in Washington."

He gave her a sharp glance, sure she was joking. "How did it get that name?"

"Well, it was painted white, but that's not how it got the name. It belonged to my grandparents on my mother's side. Their name was White. All our relatives named their houses after their last name. It was common in that part of Georgia. I refugeed to the Dailey House in Macon, named for the Dailey family."

"And when you returned home the whole world had changed." He only meant it as a casual remark, but a glance told him he'd awoken bad memories.

"I smell the river," she said and urged her horse in that direction, like she, too, didn't want to talk about the war.

They followed the fishy smell and soon the sound of rushing water filled the air. Molly pulled up to a young sapling and slid from the saddle before Luke could dismount. It sure was hard helping the lady. She seemed so independent. But what did he expect? Molly had had to make her own way for seven years. From what he gathered, her father had returned from the war a broken man and leaned heavily on his daughter.

Luke tethered Reckless beside the other horse and shoved his hands into his pockets, peering upstream where the water tumbled noisily.

Molly smiled. "This reminds me so much of the rapids back home, though that was just a mountain stream and full of rocks."

"Did you live close to the mountains?"

"No, the mountains were north of our place, but there were nice rapids not far from our church. We held picnics there often." She swung around to face him, that mischievous look in her dark eyes. "Have you ever walked across, rock from rock?"

"I've fallen in a number of times, trying, but no, there isn't a place where you could walk across."

Her mouth drew into a pout. "That's too bad. We

could have a boat race, though."

He laughed. "If we had boats."

"I don't mean real boats. Didn't you ever make little boats to race down the river?"

"As a boy." He tossed a twig out into the water. "I'm thinking you did as well."

"I was quite good at constructing leaf boats." She darted off to the trees, mostly oaks and maple, and stood looking into the dense growth.

He'd rather she not go in there. At this time of year, snakes could be hidden anywhere. "What are you looking for?"

"Magnolia leaves make nice boats. The leaves are large and thick."

"We don't have magnolia trees. Will oak do?" He reached overhead and pulled down a whole branch of a half-grown tree."

She took the branch. "It's the best alternative, I guess. We need vine too."

"Stay here," Luke ordered. He strode into the brush a little ways and came back with a trailing slender vine.

"What is it?" For all her bravado, Molly was cautious. "Some vines are poisonous."

"I don't rightly know, just a weed, but it isn't poisonous if that's what you're worried about."

"There are some poisonous vines down south, so one can't be too careful." A playful grin hovering on her lips, she plucked one of the vines from his hand. "Let's each fashion a boat. We'll launch at that place where the rock juts out. Then we'll follow them to where that big pine tree leans into the water."

"How long has it been since you made a boat, Molly?" he asked as he gathered sticks suitable for making a small boat.

"Last summer. I was alone and there was no one to race with me." A surprising sadness tinged her voice, giving him a look into her lonely life. That was something he couldn't understand. How could a beautiful woman who had so much personality possibly be lonely?

She laughed, chasing away the frown. "I went out to check the rapids to make sure it would be safe enough for the Sunday School children to wade in the cold water. It wasn't and I wasn't about to let them try it. One child drowned out there several years ago."

As she spoke, she stitched the leaves together like one with a lot of practice.

"What a tragedy that must have been," Luke said. They hadn't discussed children that much, and this looked like a good opening. "So you like children?"

"Yes, I love children. I hope to have more than

one. I was so much younger than my brother, it was like growing up an only child. I always wanted a brother or sister to play with. What about you?" A bit of uncertainty clouded her eyes.

"As many as God blesses us with. I had only one brother, but he was only two years older. I was glad to have him, as bossy as he could be at times." He held out the sticks he'd woven together. "I hope you don't mind if my boat came out looking like a raft. I'm a little rusty."

"No, all designs are permissible. Are you ready?" She sprinted to the bank.

They threw their "boats" into the churning water that tossed their creations like flotsam.

Molly grabbed the sides of her skirt and ran to follow the race. Luke gave her a head start, then loped after.

"Oh, no," Molly squealed.

Her little boat had caught in an eddy while Luke's surged ahead. A splash freed it within a second. She grabbed Luke's hand and they jogged along the riverbank the dozen yards to the pine tree, but his raft-shaped boat had already passed the finish line.

He swung her around to face him. "So, what do I win?"

She shrugged. "Bragging rights, I suppose." Her chest rose and fell from the exertion of their race.

His heart beat against his ribs but not from exertion. "I deserve more than that."

She searched his face as her arms went around his waist. His gaze landed on her mouth, those wide full lips glistening with moisture. Then he stared into her eyes shining like melted chocolate. Her magnolia complexion had taken on a ruddy hue. His gaze returned to her lips, parted slightly. An irresistible force drew him as his mouth covered those soft, moist lips.

In his dreams he'd imagined this moment, but the reality jolted him clear through to the pit of him. It took all in him to pull away from the sheer ecstasy. "I love you, Molly. I love everything about you."

She opened desire-darkened eyes. "I love you, Luke. I've been wanting you to kiss me for the longest time."

How long he held her, letting her words sink into his soul he didn't know, but suddenly the wedding date seemed much too long to wait. Realizing the irony, he laughed. The best thing to do since it released some of the passion. Kissing her forehead, he caught her small hand in his. They walked, hand in hand, back to the horses. "What will Mrs. Milton have for you to do tomorrow? I know she has plans."

"We're going to plan a tea party for later in the week to introduce me to several of her former brides—the ones who still live in Pelican Rapids. They're to help with our wedding."

That brought him back to reality. He'd hoped they would take their time with the planning since it would help him to delay the ceremony until the house was finished. As much as he wished to sweep Molly into his arms and take her to the preacher right now, he still didn't have a home fit to take her to yet. "They're planning a big wedding, then?"

"Yes, they want to invite a lot of people who'll be in town for the Independence Day festivities. I'm sure you'll know the invitees, but I won't, so it doesn't matter to me, except—" Suddenly her eyes lit brighter than the sun at high noon. She stopped and jumped in front of him, pressing a palm on his chest. "Let's tell them we don't want a big wedding. Let's get married next Sunday, right after Church services, with just the minister, his wife, and Mrs. Milton."

It was like she'd read his mind. He choked and bent over in a coughing fit, and Molly beat him on the back. "Are you all right?"

No, he was embarrassed. Truth was, he'd love to marry her next Sunday—or better yet, today. But the house was missing a wall, and the almanac said rain might be coming in. Which meant he had to get the last of his seed in the ground and work on the house. The addition didn't have a roof yet.

He came up, red-faced. "Of course, I'd love to get

married right away, but we have to think of Miz Ella. She's going to a lot of trouble for us and...I think...well...we should consider her feelings." A lame excuse, but Molly was so kind-hearted she'd buy it, even though he was asking her, the bride, to acquiesce to the wedding planner.

That lovely smile kicked his pulse up a notch. "I understand, and you're right. I owe Ella so much, and I do want to meet all the other brides. I hope to become friends with all of them. The only friend I've made so far is Mandy Carter."

He breathed easier. Mandy was safe since she knew his situation—and she'd keep Molly away from her mother. He hoped.

They reached the horses, and she slipped her hand from his and stared at the rushing water as if reluctant to leave.

"Did the rapids back near your home have a name?" he asked.

She glanced back to him. "Yes, High Falls."

High Falls. The name pierced through him, all the way through the layers of armor he'd built over the years. Luke stared at the river, unable to move as the rushing water turned into those rapids of another place, another time. When he was another man.

Molly's soft voice floated away on the summer air, replaced by a chilling wind and the shouts of drunken men.

Sergeant Lind yelled in his ear. "Where were you, Corporal?"

"I was preparing camp, sir."

"No need. I got word the general has pulled out, on the way to Milledgeville. We'll have to set out now to catch up. The rest of the men will be here with the wagons any minute, and you better have the horses ready."

As Luke worked to strap the gear onto saddles, a blast of heat replaced the icy wind. Smoke stung his eyes and filled his lungs, choking him.

Smithers rode up, a bandana covering his nose and mouth. He removed it before saluting the sergeant. "We picked it clean. No valuables left, but we filled two wagons with yams, turnips, onions, and ten hogs."

"Better than nothing," Sergeant Lind grumbled.

Four darkies came stumbling through the thick smoke. "They's done set fire to White House," one of the darkies said, the light of the fires dancing across his terrified face. "Our women folk back there."

Luke jerked his head up and stared at the flames shooting high in the sky. He'd thought they intended to burn nothing but the cotton fields. He'd set them afire himself.

"Don't worry," Giles said. "We didn't burn the slave cabins." He laughed and punched Luke's shoulder. "You won't believe what we found in one of those cabins. A piano. A big one. Filled up the whole place. I tried to set it on fire, but a bunch of old women beat it out with brooms and turned them on us. Ungrateful wenches."

"Orders were to leave the slave cabins alone," Luke said, but he wouldn't put it past Sergeant Lind to go against orders. It wouldn't be the first time. And even if he were reported to General Sherman, it was unlikely anything would be done about it.

Sparks and ashes fell around them, and he prayed the woods wouldn't catch fire. He heard the creaking of the wagons and squealing pigs before they appeared.

"Good haul, boys," Sergeant Lind barked. "Saddle up and let's pull out before the woods catch fire."

The darkies ran after Luke. "Ya'll takin all dem hogs?"

Luke swept a glance over their contorted faces. They'd just now realized their liberators were going to leave them to starve to death.

Sergeant Lind rode his horse between them. "Get on your mount, Corporal." He addressed the frightened slaves. "You men better get back there to take care of your women. They're upset a sight."

With one backward glance that would burn into his brain and replay in a hundred nightmares, Luke stumbled to his mount.

"Luke."

From far away he heard a woman's voice. He blinked several times to bring Molly into focus. His face must have drained of color because her eyes held a question. "Is something wrong?" she asked.

He swallowed the knot in his throat, and the smile he forced to his lips took all within him. She couldn't know the horror she'd just stirred in his memory, the one he'd hidden since that time—.

The White House. He'd thought the slaves were referring to the color. Yes, he'd known all along that plantation house near High Falls had burned, but there were others in the area left unscathed. And it wasn't the first Lind's troop had set fire to. But that it was Molly's home had not crossed his mind. Probably because he didn't want to believe it could be the same one. Now there was no doubt. No one else would have had a piano hidden in a slave cabin.

"No, nothing. I just...forgot something...I have to do." Like tell her he'd been near her home. Had seen it destroyed.

Helped those who set it on fire.

She squeezed his hand, sending a jolt through him. "Have I kept you from something important?"

"Yes...no. But I'd better get you back to Mrs. Milton. You'll want to discuss the tea party. If it's possible, ask them to delay the wedding until after the Fourth. The festival will last all week, if I remember correctly."

Chapter 11

Blessed are those servants whom the master, when he comes, will find watching. Assuredly, I say to you that he will gird himself and have them sit down to eat, and will come and serve them. Luke 12:37

Mrs. Milton's house reminded Molly of White House, her girlhood home. In that other world. When Mama was alive. That should have brought back happy memories. Instead the Persian rugs against hard hardwood floors, elegant furniture, gleaming wall sconces and chandeliers, and tasteful artwork, all made her sad.

The piano drew her. It was an old one, a pianoforte actually, and badly out of tune. She suspected it hadn't been played in a while. Nevertheless, that afternoon, she settled on the bench and ran her fingers over the keys. She played softly, one hymn after another, hoping they would bring peace to her troubled thoughts.

Something wasn't right between her and Luke, and she had no idea what. After their ride, she didn't see him for three days, and even then, he wasn't nearly as attentive as he'd been down by the river. Each time she recalled that kiss, her fingers went to her lips, and she shut her eyes recalling the feel of it.

He must not have been as affected by the kiss as she was, or surely he'd want to come by every day. And yesterday he acted like they'd just met. She couldn't shake the feeling he was harried, as if he couldn't wait to get away. Though he'd said he loved her, and she heard sincerity in his tone, his behavior wasn't what she'd expect from her intended.

It certainly wasn't the way she felt. She'd been giddy with excitement, wanting to experience everything with him. Get to know him. That was why she'd taken the long way to the river last Sunday. Challenging him to a boat race was perhaps foolish. Childish. But the rapids reminded her of happy times at the High Falls rapids before her world turned upside down.

Yet he wouldn't understand that. The war didn't change his world. Maybe Daddy was right to insist she find a Southerner to marry. Except there weren't enough good men left to provide husbands for the women left behind. Certainly none like Luke Ferrell.

Luke didn't share her experiences, so she'd have to concentrate on things they had in common.

But he confused her. He professed his love, but even when he'd kissed her, he'd pulled back sooner than she'd have thought a man in love would have. She must expect too much. He'd probably kissed many women in the past, and likely she didn't compare favorably to more experienced women.

The truth was. It was her first kiss.

"That's lovely, dear."

Molly started, jerking her hands from the keys. She hadn't heard Ella come up from behind. She twisted around on the piano stool. "Thank you. I hope you don't mind. I miss playing."

"Mind?" Ella was aghast. "You have my leave to play anytime you wish. I'm afraid I don't play nearly as well as you."

"Since you've been kind enough to invite me to stay here at your beautiful home until the wedding, and Minnie won't let me do anything for her, perhaps you'd permit me to tune the piano."

"You're a piano tuner?"

"No, but when Mama purchased our piano, she hired a tuner to teach us how to tune it, along with the tools to do so. I still have them. Actually, the most important thing a piano tuner must have is a good ear for tone. He said I had a better ear than Mama, so the job fell to me."

Ella put palm to cheek. "You have many hidden talents. Minnie told me you've made your own beautiful dresses and hats."

Molly grinned and tugged the bodice of her mauve dress made of fine linen and batiste. "I re-made them from Mama's old wardrobe. She had so many beautiful hoop dresses and matching hats. Many ladies sold their old dresses after the war. Had to, I suspect, but I was blessed to be able to keep Mama's."

"You did a magnificent job. Yes, I'd love for you to tune this old piano. I might be inspired to play again, though I've never played as well as you."

Minnie came in from the kitchen with a tray. "Our first guests have arrived, just coming up the steps. I'll bring them in here."

Ella smiled as she got to her feet. "Molly, I'm so

excited for you to meet Lottie, Rachel, and Marni. I invited Mandy Carter, too, since you two have gotten acquainted."

A flutter settled in Molly's stomach as it always did when facing something new. She hoped these leading ladies of Pelican Rapids would like her. Mama had been at the center of every social event in Juliette, and Molly knew these women set the rules of proper decorum for the town's society. The men might hold the titles of power, but those women held everything together.

Feminine voices rising and falling in pleasantries preceded three guests into the parlor—two blonds and a brunette. All of them stood in line to hug Ella.

After they'd all been introduced to and hugged Molly, Minnie said, "I have you ladies' tea spread out in the parlor."

"Do you have any coffee, Minnie? I was up half the night with Cora." Lottie's question had all of them looking at her like she had three heads. Molly wondered who Cora was.

"Coffee, Lottie? When you could have tea?" Minnie spoke for all of them. Apparently, coffee wasn't Lottie's normal beverage of choice.

"Caleb says coffee helps you stay awake."

"What's wrong with Cora?" Molly asked.

"She's teething, and both of us have to snatch

sleep when we can. But I have a three-year-old son so I can't snatch much sleep during the day."

"Imagine having three teething all at once," Rebecca said.

Molly almost dropped her teacup. "Oh, my. You have three children?"

"Triplets, but fortunately they've passed the teething stage."

"You two are going to scare Molly out of getting married, bringing up the trials of motherhood." Marni laid a hand on Molly's forearm. "The blessings far outweigh the trouble children bring."

"That's so true," they all agreed.

"I certainly hope it's true, since I recently discovered I'll be joining the ranks of motherhood next January."

In unison, everyone's mouth dropped, followed by talking all at once. "Does Braden know?"

"Of course he knows. I wouldn't announce it before telling him. Actually, he guessed before I did and insisted I check with the doctor."

Everyone hugged Marni again, offering their congratulations, then trekked into the drawing room and found seats.

Ella perched beside the table where Minnie had set the tea service. "While Minnie fetches Lottie's coffee, I'll pour for the rest of us. How do you take your tea, dear?" she asked Molly.

"Just sugar, ma'am." She'd never heard of putting cream in tea, though a pitcher rested on the tray. If any ice was to be had, she'd have preferred to plunk a chunk in her tea. Otherwise, she'd just as soon have coffee along with Marni. She made a mental note to always have coffee brewing at hers and Luke's home this winter. Taking the lovely rosebud china cup, she stirred with a silver spoon.

After everyone had been served, Mrs. Milton settled in her wingback chair. "Nothing warms my heart more than to see my brides in happy marriages with growing families." Her gaze landed on Molly. "Do you want a large family, dear?"

The question startled Molly and her cup clattered as she set it on the table. Naturally, she'd given thought to having babies. What woman contemplating marriage didn't? But she and Luke hadn't had time to discuss the matter much. It was too intimate a thing to discuss in letters.

"Luke and I have decided we want more than one child. I would like a large family since my brother was fourteen and already away at school when I was born, so I grew up like an only child. My mother had difficulty, and I hope I haven't inherited the problem." Mama had given birth to three still-born babies before Molly.

"Don't let that worry you," Rebecca said. "None of the women in my family ever had triplets, or even twins, yet here I am."

"I had always wished for more children, but God blessed me with Josiah and he's filled my mother's heart. Just wait on the Lord, dear." Ella's gaze swept the gathering. "You recall that Caroline thought she was incapable of bearing children due to contracting fever as a child." Mrs. Milton sent a satisfied smile over her teacup. "She and her husband adopted two children and now she's expecting one of her own."

"She is?" Marni lurched to the edge of her seat.

"Who's Caroline?" Molly asked.

"A cousin of mine from Atlanta," Lottie said. "I got a letter from her last week. I'm so happy for her."

Minnie returned with Marni's coffee and stood back. "I have a sheet of paper and pencil to take down the wedding plans." She pulled up a side chair.

"Good idea," Mrs. Milton said. "Make a note for me to speak to Rev. Lawrence and Grace about the church. We want July the third." She slid her gaze to Molly. "We hoped to have open invitations, if that's agreeable with you, but we'll reserve seats for any guests you and Luke wish."

"The only one I've invited is Mandy Carter, but if it's to be July third, she won't be here. She's returning to New York after this week."

Each woman exchanged a look among them, then Lottie cleared her throat. "You know Mandy Carter?"

"I met her on the train. She came back to announce her nuptials to a dentist in New York."

They all let out a collective breath and Marni said, "That's a relief. Poor Luke has been hounded by Mrs. Carter since he arrived in Pelican Rapids. We were so happy for him when he found you, Molly. Nothing but your marriage would put a stop to her harassment."

"Didn't you tell her, Ella?" Lottie asked.

"No, I didn't think it necessary."

"Tell me what?"

They all leaned in to her and Minnie looked up. "She'll hear when she goes to the mercantile. No single man in Pelican Rapids has been safe from Mrs. Carter's shenanigans. Most of them know how to steer clear, but Luke, being new to town, didn't and fell into her trap."

Lottie picked up the story. "She set her sights on Luke for her oldest daughter, Jenny, but Luke didn't show any interest. Mrs. Carter said it was because Jenny has a wandering eye."

"Truthfully, the problem with Jenny she's extremely shy, probably embarrassed by her mother. However, Luke liked Mandy, and Mrs. Carter pressed her plans. We all thought they'd start courting, but they never did."

Rebecca joined in. "Mrs. Carter said it was because Mandy's teeth were bad. She agreed that Mandy would go to stay with her grandparents in New York and see this dentist. I'm sure that must have galled Mrs. Carter that Mandy fell in love with the dentist."

Molly nodded. "Mandy said her parents were against the match because they didn't want her moving so far away."

Ella lifted her teacup. "Isn't that a silly excuse?"

"No, I understood. I had the same problem with Daddy. He didn't want me to leave Georgia. I want to see Mandy before she returns to New York to see how her parents received the news of her engagement."

"I still don't understand why Mandy's folks wouldn't be happy she'd found her true love," Rebecca said. "And a New York dentist must be better situated financially than a farmer." She put a hand to her mouth. "Not that Luke isn't doing well for himself."

"She doesn't want them to leave." That comment had all of them staring at Molly. She shouldn't have said anything, but now that she had, an explanation seemed in order. "Mandy and I talked about it. Her mother, maybe her father, too, wants them to stay at home, never to leave to get married. My father is the same. He was always talking about finding me a fine young man to marry—someone worthy of me. Then the man he'd introduced me to was someone who was totally unsuitable. That's what Mrs. Carter is doing. She ought to let her daughters choose their own mates.

"The problem is, for Mandy and me, we love our parents, and it's hard to break away. I still feel badly about sneaking out of the house without saying good-bye, but I didn't have the courage to confront Daddy. At least Mandy managed to do that much, so she doesn't carry the regret I do."

Ella reached out to touch her arm. "Oh, Molly, I'm so sorry you left your father on bad terms, but you were right to break away. As the Bible says, a man must leave his parents and cleave to his wife and if that's so, it stands to reason the wife must leave her parents also."

"I know it was the right thing to do, but I still carry regrets. You're all planning a grand wedding and all the while I'm thinking, I don't have anyone to give me away."

Lottie set her coffee cup down after one sip and a grimace. "Oh, honey, don't worry about that. Caleb will be honored to walk you down the aisle."

"Or Braden," Marni added.

"Thank you. You're very kind." The last word ended on a sob and tears filled Molly's eyes. She hadn't heard from Daddy, although she'd left Mrs. Milton's address in the note she'd left him and had sent a letter from Chicago to let him know she'd almost arrived at her destination.

Maybe a letter hadn't had time to get here from Georgia. She didn't know how slow the mail could be, but it had been nearly two weeks since she'd arrived. Surely a letter could have gotten here in this time.

"Ladies, would you please excuse me. I'll be pleased with anything you wish to plan and truly appreciate it, but I feel that I must...be alone right now."

Chapter 12

Is there not a time of hard service for man on earth? Job 7:1

When Luke got to the outskirts of Pelican Rapids, even Reckless wanted to turn toward Ella Milton's place. The ladies would be having a tea for Molly, planning their wedding. Luke didn't care about the details of that day except the part when they'd say their I-dos.

Frustration settled in his stomach like a rock. If he didn't have to finish the house he wouldn't have agreed to wait even the two weeks Molly asked for. He sent a worried gaze toward the darkening skies. That's all he needed—a thunderstorm. The roof wasn't on yet.

He hadn't put in a lick of work in the fields today, having worked on the roof and framing until he'd run out of nails. Mr. Jensen would expect him at the sawmill in another hour, but that gave Luke time to stop by the mercantile and buy some nails and check with Mandy on the drapes. She'd volunteered to sew them and present them as a wedding present.

As soon as the bell jingled and he stepped into the store, Mrs. Carter fell on him. "We weren't expecting you today, Luke. Mandy hasn't finished with the drapes, but they are beautiful. Our finest brocade—deep blue. Mandy's favorite color. The mister and I were happy to donate the fabric, though it's our most expensive drapery material."

"That's mighty nice of you and Mr. Carter. I appreciate it—and Mandy, for sewing them. Molly likes blue, too."

"Who?"

"Molly Stewart, my fiancée. She said she met you at the train station."

Mrs. Carter's brows rose and a mirthless chuckle broke from her open mouth. "Oh, yes, I remember.

She was on the same train as Mandy. I'd never have imagined a woman that fancy to settle on a little farm way out here. I couldn't help thinking she must be running from something. Have you been able to find out what?"

Of all the gall. He strained to keep his voice civil. "Molly isn't running from anything. She wanted a home and family. Same as me. We corresponded for months before deciding to get married."

"Ah, yes. Letters. Words on paper seem so much more sincere than in person. Have you spent much time with Miss Stewart since she arrived?"

Blast the woman. She knew how to take the starch out of him. "We've dined with Mrs. Milton and attended church." He wouldn't even mention their ride. That would lead Mrs. Carter to another insult. "I've been busy getting the house ready and Molly has been busy planning the wedding."

"Well, you'll be able to spend more time with Mandy. She'll have to go out to the farm to measure the curtains and help you finish up on the inside. There are certain things only a woman knows how to do."

"I thought Mandy was leaving last week to return to New York. I won't hold her up none."

"You won't be holding her up, dear boy. She isn't leaving."

Not leaving? Why? He almost made the mistake

of asking. "I just came in for some nails. I have to get that roof on before it rains."

"How much do you need?"

"Ten pounds should do it."

She pressed a hand to her mouth and shook her head. "Oh no, I just remembered we don't have any nails. Not roofing nails, only a pound or two of regular nails."

"What? You always have nails."

"It's been hard getting in building supplies lately. You recall those winter storms we had. Folks have been mending damage all spring."

"How long will it take to order more nails?" Luke frantically searched his brain for other sources. Maybe Dag had a supply.

"Two weeks at the earliest."

"That's too late. I'll have to find them elsewhere."

Mrs. Carter pulled a long face. "I'm so sorry. Here—take some peppermint sticks to your new lady friend. Maybe some sweets will soften her disappointment in having to delay the wedding. She does like sweets, doesn't she?"

He drew in a tired breath. "Yes ma'am, I think so, if her preference for sweetened tea is any indication."

"Let's hope she doesn't like sweets too much. That's what ruined Mandy's teeth."

He rolled his eyes to the ceiling. "Molly's teeth are beautiful—strong and white."

Mrs. Carter wasn't deterred. He should know—everyone knew—she always shot back. "They rot from inside and back. Have you looked in back?"

What? The woman was crazy. "She's my bride, not my horse," he ground out.

"That's what you say now, but you liked Mandy, too, before her teeth went bad."

"Mandy's teeth had nothing to do with it. We were just friends. Why can't you accept that? You can't just match up people the way you like."

"Why not? Ella Milton has been doing it for years."

Luke clenched his jaw hard enough to crack. The woman was beyond endurance. "Good-day, ma'am." He stalked out without taking the peppermints.

He hadn't gotten a dozen steps down the boardwalk when the doorbell jingled. "Wait, Luke."

Recognizing Mandy's voice, Luke swung around on his heel. She lugged a gunny sack with both hands. "Your nails." Huffing with exertion, she offered the sack to him.

"Thank you, Mandy. Mrs. Carter said she didn't

have any."

"She wants to delay your marriage to Molly and will try anything to do so."

"Why?"

"She still thinks you should marry me."

Yeah, that was obvious, but when would the woman accept the truth? "She said you weren't leaving. You haven't changed your mind about marrying your dentist, have you?"

"Heavens, no." She sent a wary glance over her shoulder and lowered her voice. "Just don't mention anything to Mother. She'll just cause more trouble. I'm going to leave right after your wedding—slip away in the night like Molly did."

Molly had slipped away. Didn't her father even know where she was? Maybe she had been running away. "Thank you for staying for the wedding. It means a lot to Molly and me."

She touched his shoulder. "I wouldn't think of missing it. I'm going out there and paint that music room you're preparing for Molly. I can't hang the drapes until you get the windows in, but I can paint. I'm assuming you won't have time and can't afford wall-paper, so I snatched a pail of pale blue paint. It will be lovely with the dark blue drapes and gold ties with tassels."

He ran a hand through his hair. "I'm not sure I can afford the paint, and I only have two walls up yet."

"Don't worry about that. Father said they'd donate it and the gold tassels."

"I sure do appreciate it, but you don't have to do all that."

"I'll help too."

Luke jerked to the side. He hadn't even heard Tillie Johnston coming up behind.

Mandy clutched a fist to her chest like the calvary had arrived. "Oh, thank you, Tillie. With your help, we can make new curtains for the bedroom. I bet Luke hadn't even thought of fixing that up."

Actually, he had. Just bringing his bride in there had his blood boiling every evening as he lay down. But he'd not thought there was time to do much more than clean out a shelf in the chest of drawers and make the bed. "I really appreciate you ladies, but don't tell Molly. I'm wanting her to see everything all fixed up." He sent a glance down the street. "After I pick up the lumber at Dag's, I'll go with you this afternoon and help you get started."

Tillie winked. "Don't you think any more about it. Me and Mandy will go on out. We know what to do. You got plenty of other stuff to do." She tilted her head, giving him a bird-like gaze. "Why don't you ask some of the men to help with the building? We used to have barn-raisings and house-raisings all the time."

"Everybody has so much to do this time of year with crops and getting ready for the festival."

"Posh. They can drop that stuff if a neighbor is in need."

He didn't doubt that, but he already had the house and a barn. They might think building a music room too frivolous to take them away from their normal duties.

Tillie must have seen the uncertainty in his eyes. She gave him a push. "Go on and skedaddle with you. Mandy and me will take care of everything."

Mandy put her hands on her hips and gave him a stern look. "Luke Ferrell, have you even talked with Molly about the wedding plans?"

"No, I haven't seen her since church."

Tillie's mouth dropped and she pointed a boney finger at him. "You better start spending more time with Molly. A lady doesn't like being neglected, especially not by the man she's going to marry."

That slapped him in the face. Had he been neglecting Molly? It wasn't like he didn't want to see her. She was in his thoughts from the first light of day till he dropped off at night, and even then, she dominated his dreams. It was almost like she was with him all the time. Except she wasn't.

Besides, she might ask something about the war,

and he couldn't talk about that. He would when he got up the courage and he was sure she wouldn't leave him. Maybe after their third child.

"You're right. Miss Tillie, could I pick a few more of your flowers to take to Molly?"

"Yes, I think you ought to. In fact, if I was you, I'd take her flowers every day until the wedding."

He grinned and sketched a little bow. "Thank you, ladies, for helping out at the house and setting me straight."

He turned to go but Tillie stopped him. "Don't forget the deacon's meeting tomorrow night."

His head dropped and he nodded. *Lord, I'm going to need You to stretch the hours of the day for me.*

Chapter 13

The words of a talebearer are as wounds. Proverbs 18:8

The patient bay mare waited for Molly to mount. Ella had loaned her the use of her gentlest horse, but this was the first time Molly had needed to prevail on her generosity.

She balanced on the sidesaddle and adjusted her

skirt, her muscles had just lost the soreness from her ride with Luke. The stitch in her side reminded her of why she hated a sidesaddle. Maybe she'd never learned to ride one properly, but she vowed when on the farm, she'd ride astride, wearing her habit with the full skirt that billowed over the saddle.

The day was fine and she could have walked to town, but she didn't want to stay away from the house too long in case Luke showed up. She'd been disappointed that he hadn't joined them for supper since that first day, though Mrs. Milton had invited him.

But he had much to do, so she refused to fret about it. She did fret about not hearing from Daddy. A stop at the post office was her first destination. He might have addressed a letter to the town, although she'd left him Ella's street address.

Surely after all this time, he would have written before he left for Aunt Sadie's.

"I do have a letter for you, Miss," the man behind the counter said.

Molly's heart sped. Daddy had written.

But the letter wasn't from Daddy. Her heart dropped as she spied Becky Hinson's flowery script. Becky was her friend from the Jarrell Plantation. "Thank you, sir."

Out on the boardwalk she opened the envelope. Becky's letter was short, mainly full of questions. Was Molly married yet? How did she like the place? Was it still cold?

In late June?

Becky mentioned nothing about Daddy, which left Molly wondering if she or her husband had even seen him. But one thing was sure. If Becky's letter could get to her by now, Daddy's would have also. Tears stung her eyes. He wasn't ready to forgive her. If he ever would. This was something she wished to share with Luke. If he wasn't so busy.

She took the reins and walked Burt down the street to the mercantile. Might as well do her shopping and return to Ella's. The bright sunshine couldn't break through the cloud of despair hanging over her.

For attendants' gifts, she planned to purchase plain handkerchiefs in various colors. She'd trim the handkerchiefs with white lace from one of her old dresses and monogram the corner with each of her attendants' initials. And she'd do one for Ella as well.

The empty store greeted her with familiar smells, much like the little country store in Juliette. Handkerchiefs might be in the fabric department. Anyway, the colorful calicos drew her. She'd need to sew up a few sturdy farm dresses. All her garments were of the rich fabrics of her mother's wardrobe. Beautiful, but too delicate for slopping the hogs, as Molly had discovered back in Georgia.

She ran her hand over the bolts, wondering if Luke could afford them. They'd not discussed finances either. A shuffling at the back of the store caught her attention. Mrs. Carter came from behind the green curtain that separated the counter from the back.

Molly wove her way around the aisles, but Mrs. Carter was clearly preoccupied with something and didn't look up until Molly reached the counter and cleared her throat.

"Oh, I didn't know anyone was about. You're Ella's new girl, aren't you?"

She made it sound like Molly was Ella's new servant. "Yes, Molly Stewart. You offered me a ride when I arrived in town."

The look of amazement in Mrs. Carter's eyes appeared pretentious to Molly. "Of course, now I recall. You came in on the same train as my Mandy." She lifted her shoulders and gazed around as though looking for something. "Well, what can I do for you this fine day." Mrs. Carter must have that habit of not making eye contact when she spoke.

"Do you have some unembellished handkerchiefs—you know, the type I could embroider?"

"Oh, my, yes, I have dozens of handkerchiefs." She laughed, coming from behind the counter. "Hundreds."

Molly followed the woman to a tall shelving unit stacked with sheets and towels.

Mrs. Carter squatted with a grunt and came up with a box of handkerchiefs. Molly stuck her head over the array of colored and white handkerchiefs, pleased with the selection. She plucked a rose, a blue, a yellow, and a gray. "I'll take these, and I need a skein of white embroidery thread."

Mrs. Carter took the handkerchiefs and snagged the thread on her way back to the counter. "Have too much time on your hands, dear?" she asked over her shoulder.

"No, these are gifts for my matrons-of-honor."

"You're getting married?" She swung around with a feigned surprised look on her face.

Mrs. Carter had to know about the wedding. Nothing in town got past her, or so it was said. Molly smiled. "Yes, July third. Mrs. Milton wanted it held during the Independence Festival. They're making such a to-do of it and won't let me lift a finger to help."

"How sweet of them. I fear I won't be able to do much at the festival because Mr. Carter wants to keep the mercantile open for all the visitors. That will be thirty-five cents."

Molly picked out the coins from the bottom of her reticule and plunked them on the counter. "Didn't Mandy tell you about the wedding?"

Mrs. Carter slipped the coins off the edge of the counter and dropped them in her cashbox. "No, she hasn't." She wrapped the handkerchiefs and thread in paper, folding it with a practiced hand.

"She hasn't returned to New York? Maybe she'll agree to be my bridesmaid if she's still here for the wedding." Molly knew Mandy hadn't returned to New York, but if Mrs. Carter could play ignorance, so could she. She took the box. "Is Mandy here? I'd like to ask her now."

Mrs. Carter's mouth twisted to one side. "Why, no, she went out to Luke's place."

"Oh." She ought to just walk away. Mrs. Carter was baiting her, she just knew it, but questions were crowding in. "Luke is too busy for visitors, surely."

"She's helping him get the house in order. They were always close, you know. Mandy frequently goes out to the farm."

"I see." Molly took her package. "Thank you and have a good day, Mrs. Carter."

The day that had promised to be so lovely had turned cloudy. To match her mood. She contemplated riding out to the farm, more to talk to Mandy than Luke. He would be in the fields at this time of day. But he didn't want her to see the place until after the wedding.

Why had Mandy changed her plans? Had she let her parents talk her into postponing her return to New York? In spite of Mandy's bravado, she might be as much under their thumbs as Molly had been under her father's.

Did Daddy think if he didn't correspond, she'd let her fears get the better of her and return to Georgia?

She went back inside the store and marched to the counter. "I'd like to get that lilac handkerchief too, if you please." Molly would ask Mandy to be her maid of honor. Since she would be here for the wedding, hopefully, she'd agree.

Mrs. Carter huffed like she didn't want to be bothered, but she fetched the handkerchief while Molly fished out the coin to pay for it. "No need to repackage it, I'll just stick it in my reticule. Thank you. Oh, and when Mandy returns, would you tell her I'd like to have her join us for supper tonight at six."

It was imperative she talk to Mandy as soon as possible.

It took three tries to mount Burt, but with the clouds lowering, Molly turned the horse around and headed back to Ella's.

Chapter 14

Confess your faults one to another, and pray one for another, that ye may be healed. The effectual fervent prayer of a righteous man availeth much. James 5:16

Curtis Mills droned on and on about the church's budget as he usually did at the monthly deacons meeting. Tonight his subject was repairs to the steeple and the high price of the bids they'd received, and the men could do the work themselves for much less. Luke half listened, his nerves stretching tighter with each argument against Mr. Mills's proposition.

If the men of the church didn't have time to work on the church steeple, they surely wouldn't have time to help him. But he'd prayed over it, and he was bound to ask.

"Then that's it," Brother Luther said. "We are all agreed to accept the lowest bid presented by Mr. Layton."

"Aye," everyone said.

"If you insist, I'll send Mr. Layton our acceptance," Curtis Mills grumbled.

"Is there any new business to discuss?" Brother Luther asked.

Luke drew in a fortifying breath, and lifted a hand. "I know everybody is busy this time of year, but...I...need...I'd like to ask a favor."

"Anyone want more coffee?" Tillie came from the back with the coffeepot aloft.

"I'll take another cup," Brother Luther said. "What's the favor, Luke?"

"You all know I'm getting married next week, and I haven't got the house finished yet and don't look like I can without help—what with working at the sawmill."

No one said anything, and he plowed on. "It rained in the new room, almost wetting the piano because I didn't have the roof finished. I'd sure like to get that on if any of you could spare a little time."

Questioning looks bounced around the room. Brother Luther swiped a hand over his mouth. "I'd sure be willing to help, Luke, but I don't know much about construction and I have to go over to Pikesville tomorrow, but I'll come out to your place Saturday, if you can tell me what to do."

Luke coughed in his fist. Brother Luther might cost him more time than he'd gain from his help.

"I have a trip coming up too," Mr. Mills said.

"I'd like to help out, Luke, but I'm right in the middle of replanting the wheat field," Hal Jacobs added.

A litany of different excuses followed.

Tillie plopped the coffeepot on the table loud enough to make them jump. "Now you all listen to me. There's nothing any of you got so pressing as helping a man get a roof over his head. Especially, when that man's Luke Ferrell. He's always willing to drop anything and help out a neighbor." She marched before each one on a rant. "He can't bring his bride into a house that's busted open. Now in the old days, we'd have a house raising when a young couple got married. I say we all get together tomorrow and finish up Luke's house. The ladies can fix a big meal and help out where we can."

When she finished, an uncomfortable silence had all the men squirming, including Luke. He didn't mean to cause them any trouble, and he knew as well as anyone how busy the town was, getting ready for the festival.

Brother Luther finally broke the quiet. "Tillie is as right as the Good Book. Scripture says we show we're Christians by having love for one another, and the Lord commands that we have love for our neighbor. To my way of thinking that means we help each other. I can put off my trip. I'll be out there early tomorrow morning. I'm not much of a carpenter, but I'll do what I can."

Dag slapped Luke on the shoulder. "I can't get off, Luke, but you can wait until after you've settled in with your new wife before coming back to the sawmill to work off your debt for the lumber."

Luke shook his hand. "Thank you, Dag. I'll put in an extra week to make up for it."

Mr. Mills cleared his throat. "Luke, come back by the bank, and we'll set up a loan for you to buy those cows so you can get your dairy farm started. You'll have a family to support now and that makes a difference." He laughed. "And I'm like Brother Luther, I don't know much about carpentry, but I'll be out there tomorrow and Saturday too, if we don't finish by the end of the day."

Mr. Carter came to Luke's other side. "I'll be there in the morning and donate the paint. I can paint too."

Luke about fell out hearing that offer. Everyone said the Carters were stingy, but they'd already donated paint for the inside and cloth for drapes. "Thank you, Mr. Carter. I think I have enough paint, but a second coat wouldn't hurt."

Every man came forward to offer his help. Tillie let out a hoot. "We're going to have a rip-roaring house raising—or, in this case, a house adding."

Luke leaned in and kissed her wrinkled cheek. "Thank you, Tillie. If you ever need anything, let me know."

"I always do, son. Did you give the flowers to Molly? I noticed some of the white roses missing."

"She wasn't at home when I took them, but I'm stopping by there after I leave here."

"Yes, you'd better do that. We'll take care of the work. You take care of your bride." She pressed her hand to her mouth. "Oh, I better go round up the ladies." She gathered her skirts and dashed out like she was on the way to a fire.

Luke left the church in high spirits. How foolish was he not to have asked for help before now. *Ask and ye shall be given.* Why did people not take the scripture seriously? Not wanting to impose on friends was probably rooted in pride, wanting to depend on oneself alone. But that meant he didn't trust in God, on Whom he was totally dependent.

Well, not any longer. Tillie was sure right about his need to spend time with Molly. And not only time, he had to share himself with her. Share everything. Like what happened down there in Georgia on Sherman's march.

Beginning tonight.

He turned off Ottertail Road and the lights of Ella Milton's farmhouse beckoned him like a ship to harbor. Feckless needed no urging either and picked up his pace. "You think Josiah has some oats waiting for you, don't you, boy?" Luke patted the horse's side. "I expect you're right."

Leaving Feckless to his oats, he strode the paved path to the front steps. He'd not expected to fall in love with Molly for months after their marriage. Everyone told him true love grew slowly, but now, for the first time, he realized his love had come swiftly, so unexpectedly he hadn't recognized it until this moment.

Molly was everything he'd ever wanted. She was beautiful, inside and out, kind, considerate, fun to be with, and how he loved listening to the soft cadence of her voice. He wanted to hear her sing. Play that piano.

He didn't deserve her. Why God would bless him so richly he couldn't imagine. He'd failed in everything he'd attempted so far. He'd never be a wheat farmer like his grandfather, but with Molly's help, they would found a dairy farm and raise a family.

If she loved him enough to forgive him for his past.

The sound of a piano fell on the ear, the soft notes of a familiar hymn. *Just as I Am.*

How appropriate.

Minnie opened the door and grinned. "I was kinda expecting you tonight. Come in. Ella's retired to her room to work on the wedding, but Molly's down here." She laughed. "But I guess you can hear her playing." She left him in the parlor and hustled toward the music.

The piano fell silent and within a couple of seconds Molly appeared, a smile on her sweet face. "Luke, I'm so glad you stopped by. Ella said you'd have a deacons' meeting tonight, so I feared you wouldn't have time."

He closed the distance between them and took both her hands in his. "That's something you'll never have to fear in the future, my sweet Molly. I resolve to always have time for you."

Tears welled in her eyes. "That's the most...the most wonderful thing I've ever heard, Luke, but I know how busy you've been."

He laid his arm around her shoulder and eased her to the sofa. "Not anymore. The men of the church are going to hold a house-raising tomorrow and finish the construction."

Keeping her smile in place and her eyes focused on him, she sank onto the cushions. "That's...bully, as Ella says."

He laughed and sat beside her, still holding one of her hands. "It's generous of them. Oh, and Mr. Jensen has relieved me of duty at the sawmill until after the wedding."

"But you'll still have to finish plowing the fields."

"No, I'm going to let the fields go to pasture. Mr. Mills has approved my loan to purchase a small herd of Jerseys—a start on our dairy farm."

Molly pressed her palms to her chest and then grabbed ahold of Luke in a hug he wasn't expecting, but sent a dart of happiness to his heart. He folded her in his arms and rested his chin on the top of her head. "It's going to take time and a lot of hard work, but I have my mother's cheese recipes, and with train routes springing up all over, I know we can sell all we can make to Eastern markets."

She pulled back. "Does that mean you'll let me help?"

"Let you help? I can't do it without you, Molly."

"I know how to milk."

"That's good, and once I teach you the cheese process you can help with that." He chuckled. "I expect you'll get better at it than me. Pa always said Ma was a better cheese maker than he was. She brought the recipes from Sweden."

"She's Swedish? Is that where you got your blond hair?" She reached up and ruffled his hair, sending tingles down his arms to his fingertips.

"Her hair was much lighter, but yes, I suppose so."

"We'll build the best dairy in the state. I can take care of the chickens, too, while you take the cows out to pasture."

A tendril of hair had escaped its net to fall over her cheek, and he brushed it back. "I know you wrote me all that about how you took care of the chickens back in Georgia."

"I did. I can do just about anything on the farm except one." A look of uncertainty came in her eyes.

"What's that? Muck the horse stalls?"

"No. Wring the chickens' necks. Mammy showed me before she left—and I...I ran away. I couldn't stand to see the poor things flopping around. I can put them in boiling water and pluck the feathers." She giggled. "And cook them, but you'll have to slaughter them for me. Please."

"I'll do all the slaughtering. I promise."

"Thank you. I'm sorry I'm such a coward."

The word cut through, sharply reminding him of what he had to say. He stiffened and she moved back, putting space between them. He angled to look into her eyes, like studying deep pools before diving in. "Molly, there's something I have to confess. Something you need to know about me. Something I hope you can...you'll be able to forgive."

The mood darkened like the sky before a mid-summer storm came in fast and furious. "You're still in love with Mandy." The words slipped out low and raspy.

"What?" He shook his head. "No, I've never been in love with Mandy." The sad droop of her mouth stirred his heartstrings. "What gave you that idea. Or rather, who? As if I didn't know. You've been to the mercantile, haven't you?"

"Yes, but she said—"

He took her by the shoulders. "I don't care what she said. Mandy and I have never had feelings beyond friends."

She tried to smile but failed. "I know Mandy loves her dentist in New York, but I was afraid Mrs. Carter had talked her out of it."

"I don't think so, but in any event, I've never been in love with Mandy—or any of the Carter daughters." He stroked her cheek. "I think I fell in love with you from your letters before I even met you because you wrote the words that spoke to my heart in a way no other woman had."

Her darks eyes filmed to the shade of molten

chocolate. "That's so beautiful. I hoped and prayed we'd suit each other, and I felt the Holy Spirit telling me it was right, but I didn't dare hope you'd feel the same way. Not right away."

Dropping his hands, he turned to stare at the far wall, unable to look into those beautiful, caring eyes any longer. "I, too, believe God brought us together, Molly, and I hope what I'm about to tell you doesn't change your opinion about me, but a marriage has to be based on trust. And the truth is I lied to you about something."

"What?"

"I told you I'd never been to Georgia. The truth is, I was with Sherman's army." He glanced at her out of the corner of his eye.

"Did you go with Sherman all the way to Savannah?"

Hunched over, he fisted his hands between his knees, gathering what fragments of courage he had left. "No—I sustained an injury outside of Atlanta and was discharged."

She clutched a palm to her chest. "Oh no, how were you hurt?"

He couldn't look into those soft eyes as he told her. Couldn't even sit still. Standing, he paced around the sofa. "I was under the command of Sergeant Lind, a vicious man and a drunk—a lot of Sherman's men were. His orders were to scour the countryside for food. There was precious little to be found in the towns. He turned it into a marauding party—burning, looting, and—" He couldn't tell her about how Lind and some of the other men treated the helpless women and slaves they ran into.

All strength drained from him and he returned to his place on the sofa, again clinched his hands together between his knees and stared at the floor. "I tried to get transferred, but it was the height of war in Georgia. No one could get discharged except for extraordinary reasons."

He drew in a breath, reliving the horror of that time. "I'd managed to get a kitchen detail, but Sergeant Lind informed me he needed me back on patrol, which meant another raiding party." He turned to glance at Molly, who was sitting ram-rod straight, a stricken look on her white face.

"I did the only thing I knew of to get out of it. I took a pan of boiling grease and poured it on...my leg."

Her eyes widened in horror and both hands flew to her mouth. "Oh, Luke. Were you badly hurt?"

He closed his eyes. At the time, the pain had been so great he'd retched the contents of his stomach, but he would spare her the details. Instead, he pulled up his left pants leg and rolled the stocking down.

Molly gasped. Just the sight of the red and purple scars running from knee to ankle and deformed calf making the leg looked bowed was enough to make anyone sick. He quickly pulled the stocking up.

"It's shriveled because I lost some of the muscle from infection. I almost lost the leg. Anyway, it earned me a discharge, and at the time I considered it worth the pain."

She slipped her small hand into his. "Luke, I'm so sorry."

"That wasn't the worst of it, Molly. I was received home as a hero, even though my injury wasn't battle related. I knew I was a coward, though. It ate at me as all sin does. I told you Daisy, the woman I was to marry, died. Logically, I knew she died because she got sick, but deep inside, I thought God was punishing me for my cowardice. And I didn't mention I courted Barbara Dykes for a while, but I'd started drinking heavily to try to forget and she married another. Can't blame her. I caused my parents and brother so much grief it's a wonder they didn't disown me."

He fell silent trying to gather his thoughts, to explain the miracle that happened next.

"What happened?"

"I had grown up a Christian and had believed if you turned your back on Christ, you grieved the Holy Spirit and was lost forever."

Molly shook her head, making that curl spring

back and forth over her cheek again. "No, that's not true. You can always come back. Look at the Prodigal Son."

"I did, Molly. I went to this camp meeting held by one of those traveling preachers. Somehow, he got through to me—or God did. When I got home, I begged my parents' forgiveness, but I still never told them what drove me to drink, though they suspected it was something that happened in the war."

"Of course they forgave you."

"Yes, but they thought I'd started drinking because of the general horror of war, like so many other men of our acquaintance. You're the first, other than God, I've confessed my cowardice to. But since you're from where it happened, I felt I needed to tell you everything."

"I'm glad you did. I want to know everything about you. Tell me about your growing up years. Your parents and brother. Your spiritual journey. Your hopes and dreams."

Their eyes locked. Luke probed those fathomless dark pools that showed nothing but tenderness. Did she really understand what he'd confessed to? His part in destroying her home? Her way of life? Did she even have the ability to understand the evil men could inflict on others?

Mrs. Milton's grandfather clock chimed the ninth hour. He had to leave. The stock must be tended at daybreak.

He took her in his arms. When he kissed her forehead, she tilted her beautiful face up, her lips moist, inviting. With everything in him, he schooled his passions to keep the kiss chaste, but it was she who pressed into him.

Blood boiled in his ears as he broke away. "I must be going, my love." His voice croaked, sounding strange.

Her soft whisper answered, "I know. I'll walk you to the door."

With his arm around her shoulder and hers around his waist, they strode to the door. He plucked his hat from the wall hook. "I'll see you about four tomorrow and if Miz Ella's invitation to supper holds, I'll stay for that. We'll talk about the past and plan our future."

She reached up on tiptoe and kissed his cheek. "You've made me very happy tonight, Luke. Sleep well."

Their eyes locked in a trance again, and only when the night air hit his face, did Luke realize he stood outside. *God, what a wonderful woman. I don't know why you blessed me, as undeserving as I am, with such a wife, but I thank you with all my heart.*

Chapter 15

Lift up your eyes, look around and see. All these gather together and come to you. "As I live," says the Lord. "You shall surely clothe yourselves with them all as an ornament, and bind them on you as a bride does." – Isaiah 49:18

Molly regarded her reflection in the cheval glass as tears filled her eyes. She hadn't considered how wearing her mother's wedding gown would affect her. All the sorrow and emptiness of soul that had swept through her the day after returning home to a burned shell of a home and a missing mother weighed on her spirit like a boulder.

Now she realized the war had wrecked lives on both sides of the war. Luke had witnessed the atrocities and was so traumatized, he'd burned his leg to escape, much like an animal will chew its foot off to escape a trap.

And only God could heal all those wounded by the war, whether from South or North.

"Oh, Molly, it's so beautiful with your coloring. You're simply lovely," Rebecca said. She and Ella came up from behind to fuss over the lay of the flounces.

The dress of rose-colored faille, aged to a lighter patina, boasted a lace-trimmed demi-train. The chatelaine bodice extended below the waist, and the Valenciennes lace edged the bodice and over-skirt in a quaint old-fashioned design. A wide rose ribbon that hadn't faded formed the sash, and a double row of lace frills surrounded the neckline and swooped over her shoulders.

Would Luke think her beautiful? He was coming later today, and she had to find some way to convince him what he'd done in the army wasn't cowardly. In fact, in her estimation, a man who would endure such an awful injury to get out of orders to commit horrific acts against innocent

146

people was a brave man. But she didn't think like a man.

Nevertheless, as his wife, it was her duty to help him see the other side of an issue. A wife was to complement a man, after all.

And the two shall be one.

"I have the veil." Lottie's voice came from the hallway a second before she entered the room. She held a frothy lace and net veil.

Molly turned from the mirror to allow Lottie to set it in place. All three women stood back to give a critical eye. From the looks of their expressions they weren't pleased. She twisted back around and saw the problem. The pure white clashed with the muted color of her dress and the lace was different. Besides, the thick lace of the headdress covered her hair.

"Thank you for bringing it, Lottie, but it won't work. What do you ladies think of my taking a section of lace from my petticoat—it's the same as that of the dress—and getting Mrs. Lawson, the seamstress, to fashion a headdress of flowers and lace."

"I think it would be lovely," Ella said. "That solves that problem."

Molly handed the veil to Lottie. If only she knew of a way to solve the problem with Daddy. Her hopes that he would forgive her and accept her invitation to come to the wedding had faded. "Did you ask your husband if he would give me away?"

Lottie smiled. "Yes, he'd be honored as I told you he would be. I understand you asked Mandy if she'd be your bridesmaid."

"I did. She'll be along anytime now to show me her dress. She was picking it up from Mrs. Lawson's."

As if summoned, Mandy appeared in the doorway. "Hello. Minnie told me to come on up."

"Come on in, Mandy. Did Tillie get the house raising organized?" Ella asked.

"I'll be there," Rebecca and Lottie said in unison.

"Yes, ma'am, she did. Mother can't come, but Cindy is going to bring a cherry cobbler." Mandy hugged Molly. "Your dress is beautiful. Luke is going to be struck dumb when you march down the aisle."

Molly laughed. "I hope not. It would be bad if he couldn't speak his vows." She fluffed out the skirt to show it to better advantage. "What will the ladies be doing at the house raising?"

"Feeding the men, of course. It will be like a church potluck on the grounds." Mandy squeezed her arm. "And a few of us will be finishing up inside."

"That reminds me," Rebecca said, "I've got to go.

The baby's due for a feeding, and when he gets hungry, he lets the whole farm know."

"Lottie and I will go with you," Marni added.

Ella followed them. "I'll see you out while Mandy helps Molly undress."

"Aren't you getting excited?" Mandy deftly started unbuttoning the forty-eight pearl buttons of the wedding gown. "Your wedding is just a few days away."

Yes, so excited she found it hard to eat or sleep properly, but a bit melancholy as well. Scared she couldn't live up to Luke's expectations. And she'd apparently lost her father forever. There was something else. Being the center of attention didn't sit well with her. She'd always stayed in the background as much as possible. "It doesn't seem real yet. I'm so...unsettled...I asked Luke if he still loved you."

Mandy's fingers stilled. "Why would you think that? I told you we were just friends." Behind the words was a tinge of hurt.

"I know, but your mother seemed so convinced Luke's feelings went deeper than yours—that he regretted you'd fallen in love with another man."

Mandy slid the dress off Molly's shoulders. "One thing you must know if you're to live in this town, is don't ever believe anything my mother says."

Molly recoiled to hear a daughter says such

things about her own mother. She'd always revered Mama. They had been so close. "I know it's her way of trying to control your life, but surely she does so out of love."

"Ha." Mandy held out the violet day dress Molly had laid out to put on. "You're the one who told me I was right to leave."

"But you were going to leave two weeks ago. Won't Thomas wonder where you are?"

"I sent him a letter and he's coming to get me. He'll be here for the wedding."

"Oh, that's wonderful. He'll get to meet your family and I'm sure they'll love him."

"They won't love that we'll be leaving the next day. If I know Mother, she'll try to talk him into moving his practice to Pelican Rapids."

"Are there enough people to support a dentist here?" Molly turned her back to let Mandy button her up.

"No, and anyway, Thomas has a successful practice. To keep down any friction, we'll just slip away like you did."

Molly jerked out of Mandy's reach before she'd finished the back. "You can't do that. I should never have run away. You'll regret it. I do. I should have had the courage to stand up to Daddy, even if it meant leaving on bad terms. Sneaking away was cowardly."

Mandy's face fell. "He hasn't written yet or responded to your telegram?"

Tears burned the backs of her eyes, and she swallowed hard. "No. Nothing. I sent another telegram to Aunt Sadie's address."

Mandy stroked her cheek with the back of her hand. "I'm sorry." She gestured for Molly to turn around so she could finish buttoning. "Maybe you're right. I'll discuss it with Thomas when he gets here. He'll probably want to have it out with my parents. He's no coward."

Minnie sailed into the room. "Oh, good. You've changed out of your wedding dress. It wouldn't do to let Luke see you in that. Run along. I'll put your finery away."

A surge of joy dried Molly's tears. "Luke's here?"

"Yes, he wants to see you in the garden. It's so nice out there this time of day."

Mandy kissed Molly's cheek. "I have to go anyway, dearest. You talk this over with Luke. It might be that you two can travel to Georgia this autumn after the crops come in."

Molly hadn't even considered that. "Do you think so?"

Mandy laughed as she turned to help Minnie with the dress. "From the way I've seen Luke look at you, I'd say he'll do anything to make you happy."

The happiness on Molly's face as she glanced in the mirror convinced her Mandy was right. She stuffed the loose tendrils back in her snood and pinched her cheeks to add some color, then dashed from the room and down the stairs.

She knew where Luke would be in the garden. A gazebo anchored the far boundary of the sunny space of colorful, fragrant perennials and annuals artlessly scattered about. The subtle scent of lilies, daisies, larkspur, and zinnia was overwhelmed by a huge lilac bush at the corner. Ella had already offered to give Molly a section of the bush to transplant to her farmhouse in the spring.

As soon as Molly and Luke made eye contact, he rose from the bench inside the vine-covered gazebo. His wide smile and open arms invited her, and she went into his embrace. The world fell away as they kissed.

With a groan, he broke the kiss but only moved enough to allow them to stare into each other's eyes. "Do you realize, my love, in three days it will be our wedding day?"

She laughed to relieve the emotion in her throat. "How could I not? The ladies of this town remind me several times a day."

"I probably won't be able to visit at all tomorrow, or even the next day. And Miz Ella forbids me to see you the day of the wedding until you march down the aisle." His voice turned husky.

"So, it's likely we won't see each other again until then."

His look said this was as disagreeable to him as it was to her, but she knew he'd have to work on the house raising. She'd like to tell him she didn't care if the house was finished before he took her over the threshold, but that was important to him. And anything important to him was important to her.

They sat and she ducked her head, a shy smile hiking the corners of her mouth. "I don't suppose I could join the ladies out at the house tomorrow."

"No—I don't want you to see it in the shape it's in." Alarm sounded in his tone.

She lifted her head, a full grin letting him know she was joking. "It's all right. I have much to do. I never even dared hope for my true love to marry. I can surely have enough patience to make the day perfect."

Then that old worry crept back in and she caught her lower lip between her teeth. "There's just one dark blot over my happiness."

He took her hand. "What?"

"When you were telling me how you'd injured yourself to get discharged from the army, and believed that marked you a coward...well, it reminded me I, too, have been a coward."

His brows pulled together with concern, but he said nothing.

"I have a confession to make to you, and I pray it doesn't make you think less of me."

"Never. I want you to know you can always tell me anything. What is it?"

"Daddy didn't approve of my marriage. In fact, he didn't know I was leaving." She dropped her gaze to where a yellow butterfly flitted along the sweet William blooms. "I ran away."

Luke turned, his knee touching her leg and she felt it all the way through the layers of skirt and petticoats. "You mean your father doesn't know where you are?"

"I've sent him a letter and two telegrams, but I've heard nothing."

"Could it be he's on his way up here?"

She had considered this, and the thought both pleased and scared her. "I...I doubt it." Twisting around on the bench, she peered into his troubled eyes. "Mandy suggested something that gave me hope I might reconcile with Daddy later—after he's had time to get used to the idea of our marriage."

He still held on to her left hand and she reached for his other. If only he'd agree. "This fall after harvest, we'll go to Aunt Sadie's in Alabama—that's where Daddy is moving to—and see him. If that's agreeable with you."

When he didn't respond, panic swelled. "Is it?"

"I'm sorry, Molly. I can hardly hold a coherent thought when you are near." He leaned in and kissed her cheek. "I'm more than agreeable. I think we should visit your father, but don't be surprised if he doesn't visit us before then. I can't imagine having a daughter like you and not coming to see her."

Relief and happiness settled in her chest. She kissed him and lay her head on his shoulder. With the feel of her husband-to-be's heart beating against her ear, she breathed in the sweet scent of the lilac bush. The larks sang their summer song overhead, and she couldn't imagine a more heavenly place to be.

Chapter 16

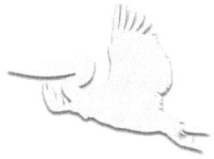

But when the king came in to see the guests, he saw a man there who did not have on a wedding garment. – Matthew 22:11

His wedding day had to be the hottest of the year. Luke stood at the front the church with Rev. Lawrence as the pews filled to capacity. He wiped his palms over his pants. It wouldn't do to take Molly's hand with a sweaty one.

As he feared, he didn't get a spare moment to see her the last two days, but the work and his tired muscles were worth it. He couldn't believe how his little house was transformed. Not only was the outside freshly painted, but the ladies had cleaned and decorated the inside. He had walked through the rooms last night trying to view them through Molly's eyes. The farmhouse couldn't make up for the plantation home she'd lost in the war, but it was cozy, if humble. He knew she'd be pleased, and nothing brought him more joy than pleasing her.

Rev. Lawrence slapped him on the back. "I've never had a bride-groom faint yet, son. You'll get through this ceremony."

"Wish they hadn't made such a to-do about it. Do I look nervous?"

"Yes." Mrs. Lawrence had joined them with her violin in hand. She reached up to pat his cheek, then turned to her husband. "We're ready, dear."

She took her place to the right of the dais and began to play Mendelsohn, and the hum of voices ceased. Rebecca and Marni came down the aisle, walking side-by-side. Mandy came close behind, carrying a huge bouquet.

Luke's pulse sped as he stared at the open doors. Mrs. Lawrence stilled her bow and silence fell until he was sure everyone could hear his heavy breathing. For one crazy moment he feared Molly had changed her mind and wouldn't appear. Then

Rev. Lawrence gestured for the congregants to stand and Mrs. Lawrence struck the Wedding March.

Water filmed Luke's eyes as Caleb appeared with Molly on his arm. She would have preferred her father escort her, but somehow Luke would win the man's approval in time. He blinked to bring this beautiful woman into focus. *Thank You, God, for sending her to me.*

She kept her gaze locked on his until she reached him, and he took her gloved hand.

The minister read the Scripture from Genesis and Luke's Gospel regarding the foundations of marriage. Luke stared into Molly's upturned face, the loving look in her dark eyes holding him spellbound. He hardly heard the pastor's sermon.

But when Rev. Lawrence cleared his throat after his prayer, Luke stood at attention like a soldier. "Luke Calvin Ferrell, do you take this woman, Molly—"

"Stop this wedding," a man shouted from the back of the church.

The congregation let out a collective gasp, and all eyes turned in the direction of the intruder. A tall, thin man with gray hair and beard stomped down the aisle.

"Sir, what is the meaning of this?" Rev. Lawrence demanded. Caleb and Braden moved in to offer assistance if needed.

"Daddy." Molly's voice was incredulous.

"You're leaving with me, Molly. This man, Luke Ferrell, killed your mother."

Shock turned to rage in Luke. "I did not. Molly, I don't know what he's talking about."

Mr. Stewart waved a paper in front of Rev. Lawrence. "Read this, preacher. Tell the whole church. This is an affidavit from my former overseer. He names Luke Ferrell as one of the men with Sergeant Nat Lind's regiment, who raided the countryside throughout Georgia. His men, with Luke Ferrell's help, burned down our house, with my wife in it, not to mention, looted, raped, and terrorized the slaves who tried to save her."

Rev. Lawrence sent a shocked look from Luke back to the enraged man. "I'm sure you're mistaken, Mr. Stewart. It was during war."

"Isn't there any decency in any of you? War doesn't excuse the murder of innocent women."

"I'm sure Luke wouldn't have done that, Daddy." Molly's voice trembled with tears. "You weren't with that regiment, were you, Luke. You were with Sherman's army."

"Sergeant Lind was with Sherman, Molly, but—"

He got no further, Mr. Stewart plowed into him

with both fists, punching him in the face, busting his mouth. Luke fell back, automatically clenching his fists. But he couldn't strike Molly's father.

Pandemonium broke out. Women screamed. Caleb and Braden grabbed ahold of Mr. Stewart. Rev. Lawrence helped Luke up. He blinked, trying to find Molly.

She was disappearing through the back door.

Chapter 17

A scoffer seeks wisdom and does not find it. But knowledge is easy to him who understands. – Proverbs 14:6

A soft knock sounded on Molly's bedroom door. "Molly, dear, may I come in?"

"Yes, Ella, please."

Molly rose from the side of the bed where she'd

been kneeling, for how long she didn't know. "I was praying," she said as if an explanation was needed.

After rushing out of the church, she'd run, the urgency to put as much distance between her and the two men she loved as possible. As her breath had given out, her spirit took over, guiding her to a place she'd be alone with her Heavenly Father, the only One Who'd never fail her.

Ella's clutched hands rested against the front of her dress, the same one she'd worn at the wedding. Like she, too, had been praying. She moved into the room and sat on the end of the bed, propping her back against the footboard. "I understand how you must feel, but I want you to know—and I know without a doubt—Luke loves you."

Molly lowered herself onto the side of the bed and stared at her lap. "I know. And I've hurt him by running away. Just as I hurt Daddy by running away." She slipped a glance to Ella. "Wasn't it Paul who said, "I do those things I don't want to do and fail to do those I should?"

"Yes, I believe it was, but that's common to us all. We'll never reach perfection in this world."

Silence deepened and all Molly could hear was her own breathing.

Ella finally spoke, softly but loud enough to make Molly jump. "What are you going to do?"

"I'm going to be still and let the Spirit lead me.

I'll speak to both Daddy and Luke. What I'll say, I don't know, except I owe them both an apology."

Minnie appeared on the threshold. "Molly, your father is downstairs. Will you see him?"

Ella reached out for her hand. "You don't have to go yet. We can offer an excuse if you wish."

Molly filled her lungs and rose. "No. I'll see him now." She straightened her shoulders as she crossed the floor.

Daddy stood in the foyer studying a painting of Washington crossing the Delaware, his back to her. To keep from startling him, she called to him as she gained the landing.

He whirled around at the sound of her voice but waited for her to reach him before speaking. "Molly, I've been out of my mind with worry."

She didn't resist when he pulled her into his arms. "You didn't receive my letter or telegrams?"

The cords in his neck bunched. "I did, but I wanted to find evidence before I came for you. I had recalled Jenkins giving me details of how the Yankees had attacked our place and what Liddy and Sam had said. I was certain Ferrell was one of the men who'd been in Lind's gang. I knew you wouldn't believe me without proof, so I found Jenkins and had him write out exactly what happened during the raid. You can read it for yourself." He pulled the paper from his inside pocket.

"I don't want to see it, Daddy." Finding all the energy draining from her, Molly turned away and strode to the stuffed leather wingchair. Daddy's steps sounded close behind. He waited for her to be seated before continuing to lay out his case against Luke. Each minute detail was like a dagger to her heart, but the peace she'd gained during her prayers held her calm.

Having regained her strength, she got to her feet and walked around the chair to put some barrier between them. The irony of having to do that made her cringe.

"Daddy, Luke told me he was with Sherman, and all the atrocities his drunken men committed, but he didn't participate. Furthermore, he deliberately injured himself so he'd be discharged. It was the only thing he knew to do."

"He told me that story too. Don't tell me you believed him?" Daddy's voice rose to a level Molly feared Ella or Minnie would hear. They might feel compelled to come to her rescue, and she wanted to have this out alone.

"Luke came to you? To explain?" Something swelled in her heart just knowing Luke had the courage to confront Daddy after that terrible public humiliation he'd endured.

"I saw his scarred leg where he poured hot grease on it. He almost lost the leg. Daddy, you know how it was in the army. Luke was an eighteen-year-old corporal. He couldn't disobey his commander."

"A man of honor would. Did he report your mother's death?" He didn't give her time to reply. "No, the whole gang of them marched off to join up with Sherman on their merry way to more looting and burning."

"Daddy, even if what you claim is true, it doesn't matter now. Luke has sought forgiveness from God and me, although I saw what he did as most honorable, and I'm convinced he didn't know Mama was in the house. I hope none of the men, as despicable as they were, knew."

"Jenkins said they did, and I believe him."

Molly threw her hands out. "Daddy, it doesn't matter now. I am going to marry Luke, if he'll still have me, and we're going to raise a family. From the bottom of my heart, I want you to be a part of our family, but it's up to you."

"Marry him? After knowing he killed your mother? You need to pack your things, Molly. Our train leaves in an hour."

Molly raised her voice. "He didn't kill Mama. Stop saying that. Stop thinking that. I'm not going with you. Yes, we're going to get married, tomorrow I hope." She turned her back on him.

"Why, Molly, at least tell me why."

The tears she'd fought rose and spilled over. She turned to face him. "Because he loves me." She held out a palm to forestall whatever argument her father had. "And I love him."

Daddy's expression crumbled and he seemed to age ten years before her eyes. He swallowed. "Then there's nothing else to be said, is there? I'd best be going."

Through her tears she watched his back, shoulders slumped like an old man, as he retreated.

She stood staring at the closed door, so lost in her thoughts, Ella startled her when she said, "Molly, are you all right?"

Releasing a deep sigh, Molly faced her with a smile she didn't feel. "Yes, I think so. Do you mind if I take Burt for a ride?"

"Why, yes, dear." Ella's voice held concern. "Are you going anywhere in particular?"

"I'm going to see Luke. He'll be out at his farm, don't you think?"

Ella smiled. "I expect so. I'll have Josiah saddle Burt. He'll have her ready by the time you change into your riding habit."

"Luke didn't want her to see the farmhouse before they got married."

They hadn't noticed Minnie had entered the

room.

"Believe me, Minnie," Ella said, "Luke will be glad to see her now under any circumstance."

Molly raced up the stairs. Now her mind was made up, she was anxious to ride. She just hoped Ella was right about Luke wanting to see her.

Chapter 18

For His anger is but for a moment. His favor is for life. Weeping may endure for a night, but joy comes in the morning. – Psalm 30:5

Tonight should have been his wedding night. Luke hardly recognized his old bedroom after the ladies of the town finished sprucing it up. They'd left feminine touches like ruffled curtains, vases of flowers, crocheted doilies. A rag rug rested by the bedside and a wedding ring quilt lay across the bed.

He had to get away from reminders of Molly. Moving swiftly through the house, he took care not to look into the new parlor where her piano stood.

Outside, the south wind only called to mind she'd left on the south train with her father, and the heavy scent of new paint reminded him she'd never see the house he'd built for her. All his time and effort, as well as that of the townspeople, was wasted.

He fled to the barn. It would soon be time to bring in Butter and Pet. He squinted against the lowering sun to search the pasture, and found the two cows lying under an oak tree, chewing their cud. Luke swiped his mouth, wincing as his hand came in contact with his busted lip.

Inside the barn the cool, hay-perfumed air hadn't changed. But even here were reminders. Feckless nickered. Luke found the curry brush and began stroking the horse's flank. "Guess it's just you and me and Reckless, old boy."

The emptiness of his futility shouldn't affect him this much, but it did, and he buried his face in the horse's neck and wept. *God, help me. I want to go after her—convince her to come back. But I'll do whatever you want me to. Just, please help me forget her.*

Feckless seemed to understand, twisting his head around to nuzzle his master.

The distant sound of horse's hooves disturbed the silence.

Luke lifted his head and dropped the curry brush. The last thing he needed was a visitor. He pulled a rag from the plank stall and wiped his face, then squared his shoulders. By the time he'd exited the barn, he could see the rider cresting the hill, coming from town.

There was something odd about the rider. He didn't sit like a man should, and as the rider reached the far end of the fenced pasture, he could tell why.

It wasn't a man, but a woman riding sidesaddle.

Molly.

She leaped from the saddle before the horse had fully stopped, and walked the remaining distance to him, tugging her horse by the reins. What was Molly doing out here? She was supposed to be a hundred miles away by now.

Her lovely face was unreadable. They stared into each other's eyes for an unbearable time. He was too stunned to think of anything to say.

She stepped forward until they were inches apart and reached up with her hand to touch his split lip. "Luke, I'm sorry."

That was his undoing. "It wasn't your fault, Molly. I understand your father's anger. I'd probably have done the same thing in his position."

"No, I'm not apologizing for my father. There is no excuse for him. I'm sorry I ran off, Luke. I was just…shocked, I suppose. I didn't want to face Daddy or the people. Or you." Her hand moved from his face, trailing all the way down his arm to his hand and slipped hers in his.

He wrapped his fingers around hers. "Molly, I didn't know about your mother. I swear I didn't. Since you told me you'd refugeed south before Sherman's army came, I thought she'd naturally have gone with you."

"Mama had planned to go with me, but at the last moment, she changed her mind. You'd have to have known my mother to understand her thinking, but she considered the slaves to be servants working the land, and she felt responsible for them. When she took me to the train depot, she told me she couldn't go off and leave 'our people' as she called them."

The first hint of a smile touched her mouth. "And she wanted to have the piano moved to one of the slave cabins because she'd heard the Yankees didn't burn them."

Molly dropped her gaze and a quiver came into her voice. "Daddy was called home and he refused to let me leave Macon until after the funeral. It wasn't until Mammy was preparing to move away that she told me what happened. She said they had just gotten the piano moved when the Union soldiers arrived, and they smelled the smoke from the cotton fields. Most of the cotton had already been harvested so it didn't make much of a fire.

"I'm sure Mama thought she had plenty of time." She lifted watery eyes, and his heart ached for her. "Mammy said she ordered them to guard the piano while she went back in the house to get something that her grandmother had given her. Mammy couldn't remember what. They didn't know what was happening until they saw the house aflame. She said the soldiers wouldn't let them go inside to find Mama, and the heat was so great, they couldn't have anyway."

"I was way back at the falls before I realized the house was afire. I didn't know there was a woman— or anyone—in that house, please believe me, Molly. If I had, I'd have gone in there myself, regardless of what the sergeant said." Despite his efforts to keep his voice under control, it croaked like a pond frog.

She reached a hand around his neck. "I know what kind of man you are, Luke. You're the man I love, and I hope you'll still marry me."

His arms found their way around her and their lips met. He ignored the pain to his injured mouth. It was the most delicious pain he'd ever known. But she seemed to become aware of his bruise and pulled away.

"When, Molly. I'll agree to whatever you wish just so long as you'll become my wife." He waved his hand in a semi-circle. "You can see the farm. It's not big. I don't have much to give, but—"

"It's a beautiful farm, and I don't need anything but you. Could we get married in the morning, early, before the festivities begin? Just us and Rev. Lawrence and his wife."

His heart tried to jump from his chest. He was getting married in the morning to the sweetest, most beautiful woman in the world. *Thank you, Lord.* "That sounds good to me, but what about your father?"

"He knows I love you and I think he'll come around in time. We'll pray he does, but I'm not responsible for my father."

He took her face tenderly in his hands. "You've made me the happiest man in the world, Molly, you know that?"

"Not any happier than you have made me. I'd better get on back to Ella's or they'll send out a posse looking for me." She turned and reached for the reins of the faithful horse. "There is one favor I'd like to ask."

"Anything." He lifted her into the saddle.

"Would you get some of the men to move the piano to the town picnic area? I promised I'd play for them—the townspeople, and I feel I owe them."

"We both owe them. I promise to do that." He'd rather bring his bride home after their vows were said, but the afternoon belonged to the town.

Chapter 19

Be glad in the Lord and rejoice, you righteous; and shout for joy, all you upright in heart! – Psalm 32:11

Molly wore the same blue dress to her wedding as she'd worn stepping off the train when she'd arrived in Pelican Rapids almost a month ago. She'd expected to find her true love here and, praise God, she had.

Ella accompanied her to the church, and if she were disappointed it wouldn't be the big wedding she and her former brides had planned, she didn't show it.

Luke's wagon with Reckless—or was it Feckless—harnessed already, stood in the yard.

When they entered the church, Molly noticed Luke and Rev. Lawrence at the front in almost the same position they'd been standing when she ran out of the building yesterday.

Someone else sat in a back pew in the shadows, and the back of his head looked very familiar. "Daddy."

All three men looked at her, and Daddy got to his feet to move into the aisle. "Molly, if you'll allow me, I'd like the honor of giving you away."

Molly looked toward Luke, then to Ella, then back to Daddy. She hugged him, not knowing why he'd had a change of heart.

Not knowing what to think, she stood searching his face for an answer until he coughed. "If you'll forgive me for yesterday."

She hugged him and kissed his cheek. "Of course I do, and I'd love for you to give me away. You have made me very happy, Daddy. You just surprised me, is all."

"Well," Ella said, "just wait right here and I'll get Grace and her violin."

Daddy actually smiled. "Molly, you deserve an explanation, but let's not waste this day on me. It belongs to you. Just know that I had a long talk with the preacher and understand the situation a lot better now. I was wrong about Luke Ferrell, and I'm satisfied he's an honorable man who cares for you."

"Luke and I will be celebrating the Fourth with the rest of the town today. Won't you join us?"

"No, my dear, I think not. I'd best catch the train."

The first notes of Grace's violin sounded, and Daddy offered her the crook of his arm. Then all of Molly's attention turned to the man waiting for her. The smile on his handsome face drew her like iron to a magnet.

"Take care of her," Daddy said as he laid her hand in Luke's.

"I will, sir."

She caught the look between the two men. Luke must have been in on the talk between Daddy and the preacher. She'd find out the details later. For now, they had made peace, and that was all that mattered.

Molly and Luke repeated the vows that united them as man and wife, and after their kiss, she looked around for Daddy. But he was gone.

She and Luke exited the church as husband and

wife and climbed into Ella's carriage that would take them to the festival.

In eighteen-seventy, the Congress of the United States had made July Fourth a federal holiday, and Pelican Rapids was one of many small towns taking advantage of the event.

Main street was lined with booths hawking their wares in honor of the Independence Day Festival, and Luke bought Molly a red, white, and blue ribbon for her hair. They had dropped Ella off at the Ladies' Quilting booth where the ladies of Pelican Rapids were selling quilts and other home-crafted items to provide for the needy. Molly promised herself to have items to donate next year, or maybe even by the Harvest Festival this year.

There were few things to celebrate after the war in the south, so these activities excited Molly as much as the children who ran from one thing to the other, making it hard for their mothers to keep up with them.

Activities abounded for everyone. Puppet shows and games for the children like the penny toss and hoop races. Horse shoes, horse races, and weight lifting contests for the men. Three-legged races, tug-of-war contests, and guess-how-many-gumdrops-in-the-jar for the whole family.

Luke and Molly strolled, arm-in-arm, toward the picnic ground where a huge big-top tent shaded a ring of horses. "Would you like to play the cavalry game?" he asked.

"What's that?" The image before her reminded Molly of pictures she'd seen of carousels in England or France. She couldn't remember which. Except those were circles of wooden horses, and these were real—six of them—whose leads were held by a man in the center.

"Diego Alvarez, who owns a ranch about twenty miles out from town, set up the game to collect funds for a library. Mr. Alvarez is a Spanish immigrant. He says cavalry is something they used to play in his home country."

"Are you sure ladies can play?" One of the boys waiting to mount the horses was a little fellow. The game had to be tamer than its name implied.

"Yes, see. The gray horse has a sidesaddle. The object is to gallop around in the circle and try to grab the ring attached to the pole held by that man who teases the riders by dangling it in front of them as they approach, then snatching it away as they get within reach. The prize is the ring."

She held out the lovely gold and turquoise ring he'd put on her ring finger just a couple of hours ago. "Why would I, when I have this? And you come with it." She hugged his side.

He took her hand and kissed the ring. She longed for him to kiss her properly, but that wasn't done in this public place. "I wish we could ride, and Pelican Rapids needs a library, but people are already spreading out their blankets for the picnic, and I promised to play for them. I hope the piano was brought in."

"It was. I helped the piano posse last night."

"The what?"

"That's what Sheriff Kouch called the men who helped move the piano. He's never had to call up a real posse, so it was a joke."

She laughed. "Let's hope that's the only type of posse he has to call up."

"Molly. Luke." The shout sounded over the noise of the hundreds of people speaking at once.

Molly searched the crowds that had grown the closer to the river they got. That was Mandy's voice, but where was she?

"Over here."

Luke pointed toward the dais set up for the speakers. "There." He slid an arm around her waist to lead her through the crowd until they reached Mandy.

Molly hugged her friend and noticed the tall man with brown curly hair and trim goatee standing behind her.

Mandy followed her gaze and grabbed the man's hand. "Molly, Luke, this is Thomas Bingham, my fiancé."

The men shook hands and Molly nodded. "So happy to finally meet you. I've heard much about you, Dr. Bingham."

"And I, you, Mrs. Ferrell. Mandy tells me congratulations are in order."

"Mama told me you and Luke got married this morning, and I'm over-the-moon with excitement for you. I prayed all night things would work out."

"What about you two?" Luke asked.

"I took your advice, Molly. When Thomas came in, we sat down with Mama and Papa and invited them to our wedding in August. In New York. Of course Mama whined, but Thomas won her over." Mandy hugged him to her. "He can win anyone over."

"Congratulations to the both of you. Molly and I will try to get there for the wedding."

"Oh, you must. Molly must be my matron of honor. My sisters will be my bridesmaids."

"So your mother agreed to attend the wedding?"

"She did. She's even talking about going back with us to help plan the ceremony. I do hope she and my grandparents get along."

"I'm glad you got your parents blessings, Mandy. Daddy walked me down the aisle, though he disappeared before the end of the service." She sent a sidelong glance to Luke to see his reaction.

"You were right about your father, sweetheart. He'll come around in time, and when we invite him back for next year's celebration, I think he'll accept."

"Thomas is going to watch the shooting contest, Luke," Mandy said. "Do you want to go with him?"

"No, I'll stay by Molly's side. I have to turn the pages to her music as she plays and it's about time for her to start."

Molly grinned. There was no real need for anyone to turn the pages as most of the music she'd play she knew by heart. But she wouldn't tell Luke that.

They said their good-byes to Mandy and Dr. Bingham and made their way to the dais. The men had set her piano on the wooden structure, and after the concert it would be moved, hopefully returned to their home today. Then the stage would be given over to the local and state politicians who'd give their speeches before the bonfire and fireworks. She and Luke planned to slip away before then.

Families had grouped on the lawn, finding what shade they could. The heat of the day had every lady fanning their colorful fans, and the gentlemen loosening their collars.

Without fanfare, Molly took her place at the piano and tenderly touched the keys. It was like greeting an old friend. Yes, she'd played Ella's smaller piano, but it wasn't the same. Luke stood by her side, smiling his encouragement. He was the only thing that had been missing in her life. Now her happiness was complete and it showed in her music.

She played a litany of classics, ending with *Santa Maria.* Ella, along with her brides, Lottie, Rebecca, and Marni, rushed forward under the cover of the applause. "That was simply beautiful, dear. It had me weeping, I do declare," Ella said.

"You two haven't eaten, have you?" Lottie asked. "We could bring you plates from our basket."

Her stomach was so full of emotion, she couldn't eat a thing, but she looked at Luke. He might be hungry, but he shook his head. "We got some popcorn and a jar of lemonade earlier. That filled us up."

"I'm afraid the wedding supper we laid out at your house last night is spoiled, but fortunately, there will be plenty left here, and you're welcome to eat with all of us," Rebecca said.

How thoughtful these new friends were. "Thank you. Yes, I think we'll wait to sample the picnic fare. Besides, I want to play some patriotic songs for the crowd, plus I have written a verse for my new home." She laughed. "I can't write music, you understand, but my ditty will follow the Foster song, *Way Down Upon the Swanee River* and use the same tune. When you hear it, I want you all to know you are the ones who inspired it."

As the crowd finished their meal, they began to crouch in closer. When Luke turned the page to *Camp Town Ladies*, Molly said, "I'm going into a lot of the tunes everyone knows. Ask everybody to join me in singing."

Luke held up his hands and made the announcement. The music began with the people singing and even dancing to the livelier ones. Then she played the slower ballads and civil war songs, both North and South.

Her fingers were beginning to tire, and she deemed it time to play her finale. The haunting strains of her favorite Stephen Foster song filled the soft, summer air. Then after the final verse, she played a chord and added her version.

Way up upon the Pelican River. This is now my song.

This is where I'll stay forever. This is where I belong.

All the world is God's creation. No longer need I roam

Way up upon the Pelican River. My love and I will make our home.

After the thunderous applause died down, everyone came forward with their fulsome compliments and to congratulate Molly and Luke on their wedding.

Molly glanced at her husband and saw tears in his eyes. He was proud of her. Suddenly overcome with emotion, she felt her own tears flowing down her cheeks and hid her face in her hands. But only for a moment. She slid off the piano bench and into Luke's arms. Regardless of who watched, they kissed. To more loud applause.

Ella insisted they take the time to eat a bite before leaving. "Better take her up on the invite folks," Sheriff Kouch said. "It'll take the piano posse at least an hour to get the piano back to its home."

They all laughed and the newly married couple followed Ella to her picnic site. Not a long distance, and Molly finally felt she could eat. Luke also had found his appetite, which was a blessing since this was one night she didn't want to have to cook in a strange kitchen.

"Are you ready to go home, Mrs. Ferrell, or do you want to listen to the mayor tell us why we should reelect him next election."

"At the risk of insulting the mayor, I'd rather go home." How good that sounded to her ears.

He hooked her by the arm and they strode to the wagon where the impatient Reckless pawed the ground and shook his head. Luke circled her waist with his strong hands and lifted her into the seat. When he'd climbed into the driver's side, she patted his knee. "Minnie says after a couple is married, the husband forgets the little courtesies. I could have managed to get in the wagon by myself."

"Really. Well, you tell Minnie she's wrong, sweetheart. In fact, your feet may never hit the ground again."

She laughed as he got Reckless underway. "Let's make ole Reckless trot. I can't wait to see the inside of my beautiful new home."

Luke sobered. "I hope you like it. It's not nearly as big as your old home, I'm sure, but it's big enough to hold your piano now."

Molly drew in a breath and pressed her palms to her cheeks. "Oh...now I understand." She slipped her arm through his. "You built onto your house just to make room for my piano."

"No, that's not the only reason. It needed to be done." He cleared his throat in that way she knew indicated he was embarrassed. She found it endearing. "I knew there wasn't enough room for...children either." He chuckled. "But you're right, the piano gave me reason enough. I just hope they got it back in place before we get home."

She stretched to plant a kiss on his cheek. "I know they will. I want to see everything."

"You will. I think you'll especially like the new bedroom. The ladies fixed it up real pretty."

She felt her cheeks burn. Now it was time for her to be embarrassed, but she supposed she'd live through it. All brides did. And the excitement of being alone with the man she loved more than made up for any awkwardness.

"Can you make this nag pick up speed, darling? I can't wait to get home."

He sneaked a kiss before lightly laying the whip on Reckless. "My pleasure, Mrs. Ferrell. I want to show you your new home."

His low chuckle sent a tingle of anticipation surging through Molly. A longing rose in her to shut out the rest of the world. To enter that home her husband had worked so fervently to complete for no other reason than to please her.

And she was ready to please him—tonight and for the rest of their lives.

Author's Note

Thank you, dear reader, for reading *Molly's New Song*.

Readers are so important to the success and growth of good Christian fiction. If you enjoyed this book, please help us promote it by letting your friends know through social media and word of mouth. Subscribe to my newsletter and receive a free e-book, *Cloaked in Love*, and announcements about future books.
https://dl.bookfunnel.com/or10xrsvje

And, most important, pray for me and other authors. The publishing industry is an important way to enlighten the public about the love of God in an entertaining way. Since reviews are more important than ever for books to get noticed, please leave a review at Amazon and Goodreads. I write only for the Lord's glory and the reader's pleasure, so I would much appreciate your opinion.

Now I invite you to read an excerpt of Book 1 of

our sister series, *Westward Home and Hearts Mail-Order Brides, Lacy's Legacy.*

Excerpt from Lacy's Legacy

Chapter 1

Montana, 1872

Lacy Avant got as far as the door and something burst in her. Tears flowed. She scrounged in her pockets for a handkerchief and, coming up empty, let the drops slide down her cheeks. She'd held up well during Dottie's visit, but her friend's happy face was more than she could bear.

Recently returned from her honeymoon trip with her new husband, Dottie had plenty to be happy about. Lacy had buried hers just one month ago.

Dottie's face went slack, then she enveloped Lacy in caring arms. "I'm so sorry. Here I've been carrying on without realizing how much you must still be hurting."

Lacy refused to give in to her friend's sympathy. She pulled back. Focusing on the practical was the only way to stem the tears. "I don't know what to do. Gramps can't keep up with the stock, much less the crops. Jim Laster and your Henry have been wonderful, but they have their own farms and stock to care for."

Dottie tugged her back to the settee, and Lacy didn't object, fearing her legs would buckle at any moment.

"You'll have to remarry, Lacy, and soon, even though it's an indecent time since Mark passed."

"Was murdered," Lacy amended. She wouldn't let anyone forget that Mark wouldn't leave her even in death unless someone caused it.

"The Lord will exact vengeance on his murderer, have no fear of that. In the meantime, Mark would want you to keep this land he worked so hard for, and honey, you can't do that without a husband." Dottie wiped the tears from Lacy's face with the hem of her apron.

Dottie's lips wobbled into a smile. "You're about the strongest woman I know, but it's not just you. Your grandparents are getting feeble, and you said yourself, Louise is losing her faculties. Bert is going to have to spend more time with her instead of taking care of the stock. Besides, you'll soon have the little one to consider."

Lacy's hand went automatically to her middle where her and Mark's legacy of love was straining her dress. "Dottie, it isn't like I can pluck a new husband out of the air. There aren't more than a dozen men in this area and all of the decent ones are already married." Her hand shot out as she saw Dottie's mouth move. "And don't suggest a mail-order agency. It took you over a year to find Henry. I don't have a year before this child comes and only six months to prove up this land."

"I got me an idea," Dottie said. "You know that lady who runs the mail-order bride agency I went to—Mrs. Crenshaw? She's in Buffalo Run for a few days. I know because she paid Henry and me a visit yesterday. She likes to check up on couples to see how they're getting along."

Lacy hiccupped. "So?"

"I'll bet she might have some young man who's just waiting for a wife. One who would jump at the chance to get a land claim by marriage, especially a claim with only six months before it's proved up. It wouldn't hurt to ask her? Mrs. Crenshaw told me she's found husbands for two women who came out west for a claim on their own."

Lacy knew women could file for claims under the Homestead Act, though she couldn't imagine how a woman could build a house and cultivate enough land to become self-sufficient by herself. Taming this land had taken everything she and Mark had in them the first few years. They'd had to borrow money, and it wasn't until the third year that the farm yielded any profit at all.

"I'm not sure I like the idea of a man marrying me for my land."

"Perhaps at first, but honey, you'll be marrying him to get a partner to work the land. I have great faith in Mrs. Crenshaw. She's so dedicated in making sure the couples she matches are well-suited. Before she accepts a man's application for a mail-order bride, he has to prove he's of good moral character and can support a wife, so you don't have to worry about fortune hunters."

A mirthless laugh slipped between Lacy's lips. "I don't have a fortune for anyone to hunt." Still, the nugget of an idea was forming in her mind. "How long will Mrs. Crenshaw be in town?"

"She'll have to stay until the next stage, and that won't be until Thursday. She's staying at the boardinghouse. I could go with you and introduce you."

No, the whole idea was absurd. "How could I marry another man and give him everything Mark worked so hard for?" Not to mention give her heart away when it still belonged to Mark.

"Would you rather Malcolm Dye take it?"

It wasn't an idle question. Dye owned the Double D ranch, a ten-thousand head operation to the east. He'd already run off two nester families since he took over from his father a year ago and taken over their farms. They were all wondering who would be next. She and Mark had a tenuous deal with Dye, but that wouldn't keep him at bay, especially since Mark was gone.

She clenched her hands into fists. Dye would never get this land. "He won't be satisfied to take my land. He'll be after yours, and then Jim and Nell's."

"Jim thinks we might be able to get the law to help."

"Ha, Dye owns the law."

"But Jim says we might be able to get a U. S. Marshal to come in. They've put down some of the range wars. It's against the law for the big ranchers to run farmers out."

"That's another thing, Dottie. How could I expect to find a husband who would come into a war?"

"Maybe you shouldn't tell him that right away."

"Isn't that dishonest?"

"You could tell him you're having some trouble with neighbors, just don't mention how dangerous Dye can be."

"If I lost another husband to Dye's henchmen, it would be on my conscience. No, thank you. At least Mark knew what was going on." Maybe he knew too much.

Dottie hugged her. "I've got to go, honey. Just think about it. Talk to Mrs. Crenshaw, be honest with her if you must. And we'll pray about it. You never know what God has in store."

Only a few dozen buildings made up the town of Buffalo Run. Lacy made the trek here once a month for supplies except in the dead of winter when a blizzard was in force. Which was often during their winters. No danger of snow on this warm, sunny day in late summer.

You couldn't miss the boardinghouse. It was the largest building, though why, Lacy didn't know. It was never full. Maybe in its hay day lots of traffic traveled through to get to the mines further west. It did have a good restaurant though, and if money wasn't tight, she and Mark always ate there before returning home with their supplies.

Just the thought of Mark brought sobs to her throat. She swallowed them, determined to think of the business at hand. Plenty of time for weeping back home. In her empty bed.

But if she found a husband, it wouldn't be empty. That knocked the breath out of her for a moment. She grabbed ahold of the post connecting the hitching rail until her breathing returned to normal.

She stiffened her back and wrapped Buttercup's reins around the rail made of a rough-hewn log.

The lobby was empty except for a bald man propped in a chair against the wall behind his counter, nodding off.

"Excuse me."

The man jumped, almost falling to the floor. "Yes, ma'am. You need a room?"

She hated to disappoint him. "No, I'm looking for a lady—a Mrs. Crenshaw. Is she in residence?"

"Indeed. She hasn't come down since breakfast, but I think she's leaving on the afternoon stage."

"Good, I'm glad I didn't miss her. Could you ask if she'll meet me in the dining room?"

"Certainly, and whom may I say is calling?" The man's proper speech sounded out of place in Buffalo Run. Malcolm Dye had run off some of the town's businessmen, too, and brought in his friends from back East.

"I'm Mrs. Avant. Tell Mrs. Crenshaw I'm a friend of Dottie Mae Chester."

Lacy turned and made her way to the empty dining room. She found a corner table and sat with her back to the wall so she could see when the lady approached.

She didn't have to wait long.

Dottie hadn't described Mrs. Crenshaw and the woman pictured in Lacy's mind was nothing like the attractive woman gliding toward her. She couldn't be much over forty, if that. Silver combs held the coils of her dark honey-colored hair.

Lacy stood and took Mrs. Crenshaw's elegant hand. "Thank you for seeing me without an appointment."

"That's quite all right. Any friend of Dottie's is a friend of mine." Lines formed at the corners of Mrs. Crenshaw's mouth as she smiled, the only wrinkles visible in her flawless face. Dottie had mentioned the matchmaker was a widow, and Lacy couldn't help but wonder why this woman who worked so hard to see others happily married couldn't find a mate for herself.

The desk clerk followed with a tray. "I bought you ladies some tea, compliments of the house."

"Thank you, Mr. Whitson, that's most kind of you," Mrs. Crenshaw said as she sat opposite Lacy. Mr. Whitson hovered, and Mrs. Crenshaw glanced his way out of the corner of her eye. "That's all for now." His scowl said he didn't like being dismissed, but he bowed and turned on his heel.

Yep, he was one of Dye's spies all right.

Mrs. Crenshaw poured for both of them.

"I won't take up much of your time, Mrs. Crenshaw," Lacy said, stirring sugar into her tea. "Dottie told me you run an agency to find mail-order brides for settlers."

"Are you looking for a husband, Mrs. Avant?"

"Unfortunately, yes, but I'm not a typical mail-order bride. My husband...he was...he died last month. But maybe I'm getting ahead of myself. You see, Mark and I came out here four years ago and claimed our land under the Homestead Act. We had only seven months left to fill all requirements for us to take ownership. But I'm sure you know the Homestead Act qualifications better than I." She drew in a fortifying breath. "Dottie told me your late husband was instrumental in getting it passed in Congress."

Mrs. Crenshaw inclined her head and took a sip of her tea. "Allow me to extend my deepest sympathies on the passing of your husband, my dear."

Lacy fought the tears blurring her vision. She swallowed a long drink and set the cup down with a clatter. "Mark's grandparents came with us, and they are both quite feeble and dependent on us...on me now. To make matters...more complicated...I'm with child."

Mrs. Crenshaw's hazel eyes lifted in pity. She reached out to touch Lacy's hand. "You poor dear, I understand perfectly. You stand to lose the land you and your beloved husband worked for."

The tears spilled in spite of Lacy's efforts to keep them at bay. She opened her small reticule to extract a handkerchief. "Pardon me."

Mrs. Crenshaw gave her time to get under control. "Your situation is quite unusual. I'm normally approached by men who are seeking a wife, and then I search for a suitable bride. In your case, I would have to search for a man who'd be a suitable match for you."

Lacy sniffed. It was too fantastic. She shouldn't have asked for this interview. "I don't think I could even...that is, consider another man as my husband."

Mrs. Crenshaw held teacup suspended, as if in deep thought. "What do you suggest, Mrs. Avant?"

Since she'd already wasted this good woman's and her time, Lacy decided to present her idea. "I understand this is an unusual case, but I'm not ready to remarry. If you could find a man who would agree to come out here and work for me until my land is safe, then we'd decide if marriage would be agreeable to both of us."

"He'd work for you? As a farm hand, you mean?" Mrs. Crenshaw asked. "What would you pay for wages?"

Wages? She hadn't even considered that. Of course a man would want to be paid for his labor, especially if the job were as dangerous as this one. She searched her brain for an answer, but Mark had handled all the money, and she didn't even know how much she had to pay.

She stared at the teapot, unable to meet Mrs. Crenshaw's friendly gaze. The whole thing was such a stupid idea. "I don't know if I have anything to pay. I'm sorry I wasted your time, Mrs. Crenshaw." Chair legs scraped the wooden floor as she started to rise.

"Wait, my dear." Mrs. Crenshaw's words made her drop back onto her seat. "Mrs. Avant, do you believe God works all things for our good?"

The question was so unexpected, it dried Lacy's tears. Truthfully, she couldn't see how Mark's murder was God's will, and so far, nothing good had come since Malcolm Dye had moved into the area. "I try to believe God wants what's best for us."

"Indeed He does. I believe God sends everyone to me for a purpose. Now it normally takes months to make a suitable match, but time is of the essence in your case. Do you have a full section?"

New hope surged, and Lacy tilted her chin. "Yes, a hundred and sixty acres of prime farmland, a crystal lake and several streams, plus a pretty box canyon."

If I could find a young man who's willing to

come work for you with the understanding that at the end of six months or a year—whichever you both decide—you would marry. Or if either of you didn't agree, you would pay him for his troubles and he'd on his way."

Reality set in again and Lacy's shoulders slumped. "But I may not have the money to pay him even if I saved for six months or a year."

"Perhaps you could sell a half section, or a quarter section, whichever is reasonable, to a neighbor—or possibly to the man in question."

For the first time, Lacy allowed a smile to break through. "Yes, if he would be satisfied with that arrangement, I would. Perhaps a quarter section for six months labor or a half section for a year. In fact, Gramps and I could manage a half so much easier."

Mrs. Crenshaw returned her smile. "I'm leaving today, but I'll get right on it. I'm certain I could work up some contract that would protect both your interests."

Lacy rose, not wanting to keep the good woman from her travel preparations. "Thank you. I'll be praying you can find someone willing to agree to my unusual circumstances. Don't bother with the contract. I'll have the lawyer here write one up." She had to think the matter over and make sure the contract covered everything, including the unusual jobs this man must agree to. Things she didn't want to discuss with Mrs. Crenshaw.

Both Lacy and Mrs. Crenshaw got to their feet, and the matchmaker gave her hand. "Very well. I'll tell your prospective farmhand or husband he can sign the contract when he arrives. I'll send you a wire alerting you of his arrival."

"Thank you, ma'am." Lacy turned away, then realized she'd forgotten the most important qualification for her farmhand or husband. "One other thing, Mrs. Crenshaw. Would you make sure the man you select knows how to use a gun."

Mrs. Crenshaw's brows drew together, obviously confused.

"It's quite dangerous out here in the wilderness."

An understanding smile crossed Mrs. Crenshaw's face. "I shall certainly take that into consideration, my dear, and rest assured, I, too, will be praying that I may find you the mate God would have for you."

God had already given her the perfect mate and then taken him.

No—not God. Malcolm Dye had taken him, and somehow, someway, she'd make him pay.

Ethan Wilkes left the barber shop and brushed the hair clippings still clinging to his best shirt. Ordinarily, he wouldn't have worn his Sunday best just to get a haircut, but he'd gotten a telegram from Aunt Milly to meet him at the Marshallville Café at noon. No further explanation.

It wasn't unusual for Aunt Milly to pass through town on her many travels, but she usually came out to the farm for a visit with Ma. That she wanted to meet him in town meant she didn't have time for a lengthy visit. But why would she want to see him? Aunt Milly was fastidious but sweet as could be.

He was more than a little curious.

A blast of noise met him at the café. It was a popular eatery and always crowded at mealtimes. He hoped Aunt Milly was watching for him because he didn't know how he'd find her.

Rosie, one of the waitresses who knew him, beckoned him before he'd managed a survey of the dining room. "Mrs. Crenshaw is waiting for you, Mr. Wilkes. This way."

He should have known Aunt Milly would take care of all possible difficulties. She was that type of woman. How she stayed so busy should amaze him, but she wasn't really all that old. Maybe forty-two in years, but much younger in spirit.

Ethan spotted her from across the room, and

she rose before he reached her corner table. He topped Aunt Milly by a foot, but she squeezed him around the middle hard enough to make him grunt.

He bent to kiss her on her upturned cheek. "This is a surprise, but a pleasant one," he said.

Double smile lines creased around Aunt Milly's mouth. "And made you a little curious, too."

He held her chair for her. "Yes, for sure. Ma was disappointed you couldn't come out to the farm." He settled in the chair across from her.

"I would have loved to, but I'm behind schedule as it is. I have a hundred clients waiting for me back home."

Ethan shook his head. The mail-order brides business was exploding. He'd thought enough years had passed since the War Between the States ended to replace the marriageable male population, but women were still forced to find mates through the mail.

He remembered how Ma and Pa had laughed when Aunt Milly announced opening a matrimonial agency in Boston when Uncle Max had passed away. They'd expected her to sell her home and move out here near Marshallville.

But Aunt Milly surprised them all. Her agency was a great success, resulting in hundreds of happy marriages, mostly matching lonely spinsters to settlers who'd moved west to claim land under the Homestead Act.

While he and Aunt Milly were exchanging family news, Rosie came up with a tray. "I brought your regular, Mr. Wilkes." She set a bowl of beef stew and cornbread before him.

Aunt Milly had chosen an egg salad sandwich and pickle. Rosie poured coffee for both of them and left.

"Would you bless the food, Ethan?" Aunt Milly took both his hands across the table, and Ethan spoke a simple grace.

They ate for a few minutes then Aunt Milly sipped her coffee and met his gaze. "Are you still interested in going west to start a horse farm?"

She'd caught him with his mouth full. He swallowed, nodding at the same time. "Sure am. You know Jason got married last year, and he and Kitty want to start a family soon, so I need to give them space."

It was always understood Jason, his brother, would take over the family farm and take care of Ma, and he had when Pa passed away. "I've been saving up because even with the land free, it'll cost a great deal to get started. Horse stock isn't cheap."

"I expect it will cost a bit, but you don't want to wait until all the good land is taken."

"I know there are a lot of immigrants coming in to stake claims, but I read there's still good farm land left further west." He blew on his coffee and tasted it. "And I've been able to save a good bit of cash and was thinking I might find a failing farm for cheap."

A lot of settlers went out west with unreasonable expectations. Funny how the lure of free land made people forget nothing was ever free. Forgot how harsh the conditions were. How long it would take to produce an income to support a man, much less a family.

"That you might." Aunt Milly set her cup on the table and clasped her hands together as though she was finished with the meal. "I just came from the Montana Territory, and land is going fast, but I might have found you an existing farm. Didn't you tell me Montana had about the most beautiful land anywhere in the country?"

His army regiment had been posted to the territory for his last two years of service, so he knew the land well. "Is this farm abandoned, or do you mean I'd have to buy someone out?" There were all sorts of possibilities. It took years just to get the soil ready for planting, and farmers had to go into debt. Most of the abandoned farms were owned by the bank but, depending on the condition of the property, it could be a bargain."

"When we last talked, you told me you'd want

me to find you a mail-order bride after you got settled. Does that still hold?"

Ethan dropped his spoon. He should have realized Aunt Milly would be talking brides. According to her every single man needed a wife, and if he couldn't get one on their own, she'd get him one. That went double for relatives.

He'd been joshing when he'd mentioned she could find him a bride, but the more he'd thought about it, the more sense it made. Aunt Milly had connections with more suitable women than he'd ever have.

"I might need you to find me a mail-order bride when I go out west, claim my land, and get my farm producing enough to support a wife."

She grinned in that sly way she had when hatching a plot. "Oh, good. I thought maybe you had an understanding with Violet."

He gave her an eye-popping stare. "Aunt Milly, I only took Violet to the circus that one time."

"Yes, but you knew her all through school."

"We were nothing but friends."

"Your mother thought it was more serious, but I'm glad to hear she was wrong about that. I always thought Violet too delicate for the frontier life."

"Yes, Violet is definitely too delicate."

"Good, because I've found a lovely, strong farm woman I think would suit you much better."

Here it came. He'd better put brakes to her plan. "I appreciate that, Auntie, but it'll be a long time before I'll be needing a wife—strong or not. Even if I went in search of my land tomorrow, it would take two or three years before I could think of marrying."

"You don't understand what you need a wife for, Ethan. A wife is a man's help mate to build your life together. From the beginning. A man needs a wife beside him to help plow—or take care of the horses."

It'd be useless to argue the reasons for a wife with Aunt Milly. "I'll give that some thought." He lifted his cup for a long swig, wishing it were stronger.

"The young woman I have in mind already has a farm in Montana, a lovely spread with only six months until it's proved."

Ethan almost choked on his coffee. As soon as he caught his breath, he said in a croaking voice. "You found an unmarried woman with a farm? Of her own?"

Sadness clouded Aunt Milly's features. "Yes, dear. Lacy Avant. Her husband died recently, leaving her the farm and his elderly grandparents to care for. She's a hard working woman, but needs a husband quickly, as you can imagine. Of course she wouldn't have any problem getting prospects. What man wouldn't jump at the chance to gain his own land with only a few months before it's free and clear and a good wife to boot? But she doesn't have the time to search for someone who'll treat her well. Her situation is quite desperate, really."

"That sounds desperate all right, but why did you think of me?"

She reached over to squeeze his hand. "Because I know you would treat her well, and as I was traveling to Marshallville, I felt the Lord bringing your situation to my attention. I admit I don't know Lacy well, but I have keen discernment, and I believe she would grow to love you as you deserve to be loved."

Ethan scratched his ear where some loose hair clippings were trapped. "I appreciate you thinking of me, Auntie, but the truth is, I never imagined marrying a widow, especially so soon after her husband died. That would be...awkward at best."

"I won't lie to you. Of course Lacy is still grieving, but time will heal that ache she has now. In the meantime, her circumstances demand a living husband now."

"What does she look like?" Not that it mattered, since he couldn't just pull up roots and leave on the next train to marry a desperate widow to save her farm.

"I'd say she's a couple of inches taller than I am with hair the color of ripe corn and beautiful amber eyes. Her hands are red and calloused, as you might expect a hard-working farm woman's to be."

"She sounds pretty, but honestly, Aunt Milly, I'd feel bad to move into a home that another man worked for, take his wife. His farm. As sad as it is, it would be better for this woman to sell out and move to town."

"You won't be taking her deceased husband's land, dear. If Lacy agrees to marry you, you'll be sharing the farm with her. Remember, she worked as hard for the land as her husband did. It belongs to her now, and she naturally wants to keep it."

The urge to argue was still strong. "I'm intrigued, but you know I have to help Jason with harvesting this time of year."

Aunt Milly's lips pressed together in a stubborn line before she spoke. "Jason wouldn't want you to give up an opportunity for happiness. Besides, he can hire help. Which brings me to the most intriguing part of Lacy's proposal. She doesn't want to marry right away, rather she suggests the prospective groom work for her, and if they decide not to marry, she'll give him a quarter section for six months of labor or a half section for a year. I didn't see her home, but the land surrounding Buffalo Run is lovely."

"I know. I've been through that town a couple of times. It's not far from the mountain range."

She fiddled with her napkin, folding it into a neat square. "But if you should marry, as I hope you might, you'd share the full section. Lacy promised to have a contract prepared to cover those details." She tapped the table between them. "Oh, and her grandparents live with her, so there will be no problem with you taking a room in the house while you work the farm."

Aunt Milly and Lacy had certainly covered all possible objections. The proposition sounded too good to be true, and he'd have to see the property first—as well as Lacy.

And think about it. He needed time to think.

Silence fell between them as he finished his stew.

Aunt Milly examined her watch. "I must go. My train will be leaving within a few minutes. Will you think about my proposition, Ethan, and send me a telegram by Friday if you decide to at least go out to meet Lacy?"

"Sure, I'll let you know, and I truly do appreciate you stopping by to see me." His chair tipped back in his haste to stand. He righted it, then pulled her chair out and walked her to the train depot, which was next door to the café.

The train was already boarding. Ethan followed

her to the depot's platform. Something didn't feel right, and he was strangely reluctant to see her depart.

She turned to face him. "You were a sharp-shooter in the Calvary, weren't you, dear?"

"You know I was. Ma fussed about it enough."

"I suppose I worried about the danger you were in, too, and the west is still a dangerous place. In fact, I thought of you when Lacy mentioned wanting a man who could handle a gun."

He wanted to ask her more about that, but she pulled him into a sideways hug, and he knew there wasn't enough time.

"Give my regards to Jason and Kitty and your dear mother."

"I will." He dropped a kiss on her cheek. "Safe travels, and I hope you can stay longer next time."

She smiled and pivoted to the gesturing porter. Ethan turned on his heel and had covered several steps when Aunt Milly's voice jerked him around. "Ethan, I forgot one detail." She crooked a finger for him to return.

He retraced his steps. Aunt Milly lifted a hand to shield her words.

"She's with child."

He stood stock still, glued to the platform. He couldn't force himself to turn away, even as she disappeared into the train.

Oddly, a memory of his father flashed through his mind. Ethan had been nine years old, just questioning his purpose in life, a little afraid of things he'd learned at Church about his eternal soul. "Pa, I've done all the preacher said, confessed and believe, but how will I know if I'm a Christian?" he'd asked.

Pa had chewed on a sprig of hay for several moments before answering. "You remember the parable of the Good Samaritan?"

"Yes sir, he was the one who stopped to help that fellow who was in a pickle when everyone else walked by."

Pa had patted him on the shoulder. "That's right, son, you remember good." He'd walked away, leaving Ethan confused.

What kind of answer was that? Ethan ran after him. "How does that tell me anything? How will I know if I'm a Christian?"

Pa had squatted to get at eye-level and took him by the shoulders. "'Cause you'll be the one who stops. You'll be the one who reaches out to help that fellow in a pickle."

Simple words from a simple man, but so profound they'd clung to Ethan and shaped his understanding of Christian duty better than anything since. His pa was a wise man, and now that he was gone, Ethan was beginning to realize just how wise.

Lacy's child wouldn't have a father.

Who would need help more than a woman carrying a baby and trying to run a farm by herself? Was it possible that God wanted him to help this widow? And if so, how could he refuse?

Then Aunt Milly appeared in a window, a dozen back. She smiled and waved. The doors closed. The train's engine chugged as steam billowed, momentarily obscuring his vision.

He ran along the side until he was level with Aunt Milly's window. Holding his hand to his mouth, much as she'd done earlier—not to prevent anyone from hearing but to be heard above the noise. "Aunt Milly," he shouted, "go ahead and send Lacy a telegram. Tell her I'll come within a week, and if she wants me, I'll marry her."

That earned him a lot of curious stares, but who cared. These people were just traveling through. And even if one of the locals who knew him had heard, it didn't matter.

He'd be in Montana. With Lacy and her child.

Books by this Author

The Annex Mail Order Brides series:
Adela's Prairie Suitor
Ramee's Fugitive Cowboy
Prudie's Mountain Man
The Annex Mail-Order Brides Boxset

Intrigue under Western Skies series:
Book 1, Pursued
Book 2, Surrendered
Book 3, Revealed
Book 4, Escaped

The Wolf Deceivers series:
Book 1, The Chieftain's Choice
Book 2, The Duke's Dilemma
Book 3, The Captain's Challenge

Westward Home and Hearts, a mult-author series:
Book 1, Lacy's Legacy
Book 3, Maggie's Christmas Miracle

Brides of Pelican Rapids, a mult-author series:

Book 5, Molly's New Song

Also:

The Perfect Gift, a Christmas Novella
The Washwoman's Christmas
Cloaked in Love

About the Author

Elaine Manders writes wholesome, Christian romance about the strong, capable women of history and present day and the men who love them. She lives in Central Georgia with a happy bichon-poodle mix. When not writing, she enjoys reading, sewing, crafts, and spending time with her daughter, grandchildren, and friends. You may contact the author at any of the following.

Facebook:
https://www.facebook.com/elaine.manders.35
Twitter: https://twitter.com/ehmanders
Email: elainehmanders@gmail.com
Bookbub:
https://www.bookbub.com/authors/elaine-manders
Goodreads:
https://www.goodreads.com/author/show/14151675
.Elaine_Manders

www.ingramcontent.com/pod-product-compliance
Lightning Source LLC
Chambersburg PA
CBHW032120170626
46808CB00006B/2031